CAPRA BACK-TO-BACK SERIES

The Man Who Cultivated Fire

In these stories, Haslam portrays rural people struggling to make something of themselves and to live with dignity in the raw American West. Most of these tales are set in what critics have called "the other California"—poor, tough, crafty, and often desperate.

GERALD HASLAM comes from the oilfields and ranches of the Great Central Valley and is known primarily for his short stories. His first collection, *Okies,* was published in 1975. With James D. Houston, he edited *California Heartland* for Capra Press in 1978.

The Back-to-Back Series provides a showcase for shorter literary work from both established and newer writers and is published by

CAPRA PRESS

POST OFFICE BOX 2068, SANTA BARBARA, CALIFORNIA 93120

VOLUME XI
CAPRA BACK-TO-BACK SERIES

Prettyfields

PRETTYFIELDS depicts a gang of irreverent students at a New England academy in the late thirties. They assail the boundaries between literature, reality, and imagination with Rabelesian fervor.

WILLIAM EASTLAKE is best known for his series of novels set in New Mexico's Indian country. He lives and writes in Arizona.

*The Back-to-Back Series provides a showcase
for shorter literary work from both established
and newer writers and is published by*

CAPRA PRESS

POST OFFICE BOX 2068, SANTA BARBARA, CALIFORNIA 93120

THE CAPRA BACK-TO-BACK SERIES

1. URSULA K. LE GUIN, The Visionary *and*
   SCOTT R. SANDERS, Wonders Hidden

2. ANAÏS NIN, The White Blackbird *and*
   KANOKO OKAMOTO, The Tale of an Old Geisha

3. JAMES D. HOUSTON, One Can Think About Life
   After the Fish is in The Canoe *and*
   JEANNE WAKATSUKI HOUSTON, Beyond Manzanar

4. HERBERT GOLD, Stories of Misbegotten Love *and*
   DON ASHER, Angel on My Shoulder

5. RAYMOND CARVER and TESS GALLAGHER,
   Dostoevsky (The Screenplay) *and*
   URSULA K. LE GUIN, King Dog (A Screenplay)

6. EDWARD HOAGLAND, City Tales *and*
   GRETEL EHRLICH, Wyoming Stories

7. EDWARD ABBEY, Confessions of a Barbarian *and*
   JACK CURTIS, Red Knife Valley

8. ROBERT COOVER, Aesop's Forest *and*
   BRIAN SWANN, The Plot of the Mice

9. LEW AMSTER, The Killer Instinct *and*
   SANORA BABB, The Dark Earth

10. THOMAS SANCHEZ, Angels Burning *and*
    LAWRENCE CLARK POWELL, "Ocian in View"

11. WILLIAM EASTLAKE, Prettyfields *and*
    GERALD HASLAM, The Man Who Cultivated Fire

WILLIAM EASTLAKE

Prettyfields

A Work in Progress

VOLUME XI

CAPRA PRESS

1987

Cover design by Francine Rudesill.
Designed and typeset in Garamond by Jim Cook
SANTA BARBARA, CALIFORNIA

LIBRARY OF CONGRESS CATALOGING-IN-PUBLICATION DATA
Eastlake, William.
Prettyfields: a work in progress.
(Capra back-to-back; v. 11)
No collective t.p. Titles transcribed from individual title pages.
Texts bound together back to back and inverted.
I. Haslam, Gerald W. Man who cultivated fire, and other stories. 1987.
II. Title.   III. Title: Man who cultivated fire, and other stories.
PS3555.A7P7 1987   813'.54   87-11791
ISBN 0-88496-266-0 (pbk)

PUBLISHED BY
CAPRA PRESS
Post Office Box 2068
Santa Barbara, California 93120

PRETTYFIELDS

Prettyfields

I

IN THE DARK NIGHT OF THE SOUL IT IS ALWAYS THREE O'CLOCK IN THE MORN-ING.—F. SCOTT FITZGERALD. That's what our teacher Elizabeth Mary Coca wrote in tall white chalk letters on the blackboard, and after class we wrote beneath it, E. MARY COCA LOVES F. SCOTT FITZGERALD.

Miss Coca taught creative writing at our northern New Jersey Episcopalian boys school called Prettyfields, taught writing in the rife green and gentle roll of the undulating hills that Walt Whitman called his home and Stephen Crane quit to go to wars. Miss Coca said creative writing could not be taught.

"Then why do you teach it?"

"In the hope that a child genius will come along, an incipient genius who can be encouraged. You can't teach genius, but you can encourage it, nurture its growth, you might say spread concern on the surprising flower."

7

Miss Coca thought about this while staring at the pictures of Ernest Hemingway, John Dos Passos, Thomas Wolfe, Walt Whitman, Stephen Crane, Emily Dickinson and William Faulkner that decorated the walls of the dark and heavy oak-beamed creative writing room.

Miss Coca taught us to be suspicious of any book that sold over five thousand copies, that a book without a moral center had no survival value, that a bad novel was the longest distance between two points.

"What's that mean?"

"Think about it."

She taught us that Margaret Mitchell's *Gone With the Wind* was a southern Civil War soap opera.

"Did that sell more than five thousand copies?"

"I think so."

That although there were a lot of poets, there was no poetry, that all great novelists wrote poetic novels.

"Like who?"

"Herman Melville."

"Like what?"

"Moby Dick."

"Bartleby the Scrivener?"

"Yes."

"Is that all for the day?"

"Remember that in the novel the truth of the matter is the concealment of the virtuous lie. You are putting on a magic show."

"What's that mean?"

"Think about it."

Sometimes Miss Coca seemed to have a sense of humor and

then she would lose it. When she had it, she said Ernest Hemingway was not thinking of the pilots in World War One who started their planes by swinging their propellers by hand when he called his book *A Farewell to Arms*. Miss Coca lost her sense of humor when Clancy walked in front of her one cold, breezy day and said he would break wind for her—she didn't think that was funny at all.

One day Eddie told Miss Coca he had relatives who were in the war and they didn't talk like the soldiers in Ernest Hemingway's *Farewell to Arms*.

"You mean Hemingway's soldiers didn't use filthy language?"

"Maybe my uncle went to a different war."

Miss Coca stared at Ernest Hemingway and at all the other authors on the wall who had not said it as it was spoken, but Ernest had promised he was telling it "truly." The other writers had kept their mouths shut about telling it as it is not. Of all the authors on the wall, Miss Coca thought Emily Dickinson the most honest. There was an excellent chance that, cooped up in her father's many-gabled New England house, she had never heard the language of the bedroom, the street or the army. Emily was the only one who said it as she knew it to be. She spoke the true language of her mind and her heart. Ernest had deceived the world because although he had claimed otherwise, he wrote to fit the book not the life. F. Scott Fitzgerald, along with Emily Dickinson, may have been protected from the real of life by having lived with the academic and the rich. Yet Scott was an honest writer. But too slick. Too high-paying ladies' magazines. But F. Scott Fitzgerald, unlike Ernest, wrote honestly of what he knew. "But he didn't know much," Clancy Nublood said.

"Very little," Eddie Markowitz said.

Miss Mary Coca put down the white chalk with which she had written F. Scott Fitzgerald on the blackboard and said, "That is your opinion, Edward." And she wondered when she went to her chair why Edward Teodor Markowitz had not, like Joseph Conrad, changed his Polish name into something more literary. Yes, Joseph Conrad's name had been Teodor Jozef Konrad Korzeniowski before he invented a much more spellable one. It was difficult for Miss Coca to think of anything at all except in literary thoughts. She realized now that her affection for Ernest Hemingway was slipping away and she was drifting ever closer to F. Scott Fitzgerald.

"You think so?"

"I know so."

"Why don't we, Bill," Clancy said to me, "hide with your recorder outside Miss Coca's room and collect all of her crazy life?"

My wire recorder preceded the tape recorder and the computer, the computer that led to the downfall of all civilization and Texas.

"Because it wouldn't be ethical," I said.

"Ethical, bethical. Why not, Bill? How can you get an oral history of mankind and leave out women?"

"It's not all of mankind, it's just Prettyfields, but you have a point."

"Not only that, Bill. We can sit on the mansard roof outside her window and see her to," Clancy said.

"Her act?"

"Yes."

And we did, because youth is cruel. The young are unkind. We did it just as Miss Coca was breaking up with Ernest Hemingway and drifting into a liaison with F. Scott Fitzgerald. It had not turned into an affair yet with Scott, but it was getting close.

"Damn close," Clancy sitting in the darkness said.

E. Mary Coca had F. Scott Fitzgerald's picture on her nightstand. This was new. Howard Tordiff had delivered a package to her room a week ago and Scott was not there then. Miss Coca was a virgin. We all were. But Miss Coca was an old lady. Miss Coca must have been thirty. But if Miss Coca considered us to be very young, which we did not consider ourselves to be, then we could consider her very old, which she did not consider herself to be. It was a Mexican stand-off. Miss Coca had grown up in Boston which gave her a foreign accent. She said clam chowda for clam chowder and hahses for horses, Bahston for Boston. She said Paul Reveeah had the fahstest hahse in Bahston. But after awhile you could make out what she was trying to say.

How are boys to know the quiet terror of a lost spinster lady's loneliness, her vale of despair in the far green hills of not home, not city, not sex? All she had in her life at Prettyfields was the arrogance of children, the voices of Franklin D. Roosevelt and H. V. Kaltenborn on her radio, the book section of the Sunday "New York Times" in her magazine rack, and F. Scott Fitzgerald at her bedside.

Miss Coca wore a peekaboo boy's bob, rosebud lips, short, tight pink skirt, and pink silk stockings rolled at the top above black Flapper galoshes she affected when it did not rain. She came into the bedroom now and said, "Hi, Scott." She hung her coat in the closet. "How is *Tender Is the Night* going? I read your *Diamond as Big as the Ritz* to the class today. I don't think they understood it. Bill Faulkner dropped by and Hemingway called while you were

out. Hem sounds tired and bitter and old. Hem's problem is he's
lost respect for himself while he's still in love with himself." She
rearranged the flowers on the dressing table. "Hem wanted to
know what you thought of *Snows*. You're supposed to know he
means his short story, *The Snows of Kilimanjaro* where he called
you his favorite rummy. *Snows* is the story where you are
supposed to have said, "Ernest, the rich are different than you and
me," and then he gave himself the line, "Yes, they got more
money." She looked around the room. "You've made a mess of
things, Scott," she said, picking imaginary clothes off the floor and
hanging them in the closet. "Hem is having a feud with Gertrude.
She called him a Rotarian and he came back with 'lesbian.' "

"What's that?" Howie Tordiff said.

"Well, that's the gossip, Scott. Wait while I get the phone."
When Miss Coca got the phone she said, "Oh, hi, Tom." Then she
put her hand over the mouthpiece and said over to Scott, "It's
Thomas Wolfe. Are you in?" Then into the mouthpiece, "No, he's
not, Tom. What's on your mind? Well, I wouldn't let the critics
bother me. Don't read the critics, Tom. If you believe the critics
when they say you are good, you will believe then when they say
you are bad. Then you wouldn't write, Tom. I just talked to Hem.
He's not writing. No, that's not good, Tom. Have you heard from
Eugene O'Neill? Gene's in a funk over the pan George Jean
Nathan gave *The Iceman Cometh*. No, I didn't see it. I don't see
anything at Prettyfields. No, Tom, there isn't anyone to talk to at
Prettyfields."

"What about us?" Raymond Hall said.

"Tell me, Tom, have you found America yet? You lost it in *You
Can't Go Home Again* and almost got hold of it in *Look*

Homeward, Angel. That's mighty powerful poetry, Tom. We all love you for it. I love you for it. Am I lonely here at Prettyfields? Yes, Tom, and I do, do appreciate your call. I appreciate your concern very much. I do, I do. Listen, Tom, I've got to buzz off. Scott is having trouble with *The Last Tycoon.* No, that's the title of his new book. He is having trouble with Scribner's. Sales of *The Great Gatsby* are down to zero. We may have to pack it off to Hollywood. No, I won't go now. I have my creative writing class here that I can't run out on. I may join Scott in Hollywood later."

"You may, may you?" Raymond Hall said.

"I've got to run now, Tom. Give my love to Aline Bernstein. Yes, I'll tell Scott that. Bye bye, Tom." Miss Coca hung up. "That was Wolfe. He wanted me to tell you that that part of America that was lost has been found. No, I don't think it's corny, Scott. No, I don't think it's adolescent. If you say that, then you can say that all poetry is adolescent, all love, all feeling, all that is deep and abiding, all heart-felt emotion is adolescent. You don't want to say that, Scott. I don't want to quarrel again, Scott. Growing up does not mean the abandoning of the beauty and the poetry in life. No, I'm not accusing you again of drinking too much, although I do think you should cut down. No, I'm not saying you should go back to Zelda."

"Who's Zelda?" Raymond said.

"What I am saying is, Scott, Hollywood is not worthy of you. Hollywood will destroy you, Scott. That's right. It didn't destroy Faulkner, but you're not Faulkner. You're F. Scott Fitzgerald, and don't ever forget that. The world will never forget that, because the world will never forget *The Great Gatsby.* Because I won't let them, Scott. No, I can't go to Hollywood now. I have my responsibilities to my creative writing class. Do I have any good students? Yes, William Catchfield."

I got an elbow in the ribs and some giggles.

"He's a cripple. No, it's not my mothering instinct he appeals to, it's his talent. No, I don't think he'll make it as a writer. He doesn't have enough drive. But people with drive bore me, Scott. All the best-sellers are made by people with drive. If you had drive, Scott, you wouldn't be going off to Hollywood. You're quitting, Scott, running out on us. Don't throw that lamp, Scott." Miss Coca crouched behind her settee. "Don't, Scott. Don't. My God, he slammed the door. He ran out on me," she said.

Now Elizabeth Mary Coca sat on the bed's pink counterpane and stared down at her feet as though they might have some message as to what to do when you are a prisoner at Prettyfields. Ballet. She darted up and stripped off her blouse, then her skirt, then everything was at her feet in front of the full-length mirror. She tried to get on her toes, twirled her body, examined herself.

Pete Nelson touched his chin. "Not bad."

Raymond Hall leaned forward. "Dance," he said.

Miss Coca reached for the pink counterpane, draped the pink counterpane around her same-pink body in a swirling gesture, then danced to the light of the moon, the light of our eyes.

"Delight of our eyes," Eddie said.

"Jesus Christ," Clancy said.

Raymond Hall touched his head in the moon. "Very en garde in feeling."

Howard Tordiff scratched his rear end and spat, then contemplated. "You think so?"

"I know so." Raymond Hall tilted closely in the moonshadow.

"She had one gorgeous moment, one marvelous moment in tone. It's a private dance in the worst sense, but because of its imagination, private in the best sense too. She has invested her contretemps with some rudimentary but enchanting inversions of port de bras—"

"Oh, Jesus Christ," Clancy said.

Miss Coca flung off her counterpane and danced in the lightness of nothing.

"Oh, wow!"

Miss Coca declaimed to the moon, to our moon shadows,

"In Prettyfields did Kubla Khan
A stately pleasure-dome decree
Where Blue, the sacred river, ran
Through caverns measureless to man
Down to the sunless sea . . .
And there were gardens bright with sinuous rills,
Where blossomed many an incense-bearing tree,
And here were forests ancient as the hills,
Enfolding sunny spots of greenery.

But oh! . . .
A savage place! as holy and enchanted
As e'er beneath a waning moon was haunted
By woman wailing for her demon-lover!

. . . And all who heard should see them there,
And all should cry, Beware! Beware!
His flashing eyes, his floating hair!

Weave a circle round me thrice,
And close my eyes with holy dread,
For he on honey-dew hath fed,
And drunk the milk of Paradise."

SHE HELD HERSELF on tiptoe now, almost en pointe. "Take me, take me. Consummate. Consummate."

"I think that's some kind of soup," Gregory said.

"Could be."

"Barbarians," Raymond Hall said.

Now Miss Coca accomplished her ultimate movement in her pas de deux, she solo, but bowing big to her phantom partner.

"Both bare-assed."

"Yes."

Then bowed to our unseen but not unseeing moon crowd.

"Bravo," Raymond Hall heavy-whispered. "Bravo."

"Let's go," Pete Nelson said. "The show was a waste of money, but it was worth it."

"The hell it was," Clancy said.

Round about three weeks later, Miss Coca was taken off to the booby hatch. Just like that. Without a faretheewell. Without a leaving. Without anything. Adults do things without ever considering the students. Without consulting the young victims. In those days they called it a nervous breakdown and packed Miss Coca off to the Overbrook Sanitarium. They packed her off without consulting Dr. Forest. "Yes, I believe Miss Coca is crazy," Dr. Forest said from his seat in his Packard, "and I believe I am crazy and Franklin D. Roosevelt is crazy and every person who believes in the dream—that includes Roosevelt's wife, Eleanor.

During the uncivil war, the entire North was crazy because they believed that fourscore and seven years ago there was created on this continent a new nation conceived in liberty and dedicated to the proposition that all men are created equal. A million men risked their lives to prove that. I lost many friends, many friends, many dear comrades. *When lilacs last in the dooryard bloom'd.* Did I tell you I saw Lincoln plain?"

"It was Whitman. You said you only saw Lincoln from the rear."

"When our column turned on Pennsylvania Avenue, for a quick second I saw Lincoln plain."

"Doctor Forest, what we want to know is what is going to happen to Miss Coca?"

Dr. Forest got out of the front seat of the Packard touring car and sat with us on the running board and stroked his beard, his eyes remote and lost as though cogitating Grant's encircling movement against Vicksburg, but although lost he was dwelling on our question.

"I believe more of my comrades were lost to insanity rather than bullets. Those that fight and run away, live to die another way. Did Miss Coca have you read Stephen Crane's *The Red Badge of Courage?*"

"Yes."

"That was a daisy," Dr. Forest said. "Where does that leave your Ernest Hemingway?"

"I believe he's in Spain. Miss Coca told us he's writing more about bullfighting."

"That's sick." Dr. Forest opened the toolbox on the running board and searched for a cigar and found one, a ten-cent Cremo. A

Cremo was the first cigar that came with a hole in the mouth end so you didn't have to bite it off. Their ad was, "Spit is a horrid word." Dr. Forest lit up and said, "Wrong, boys."

"Miss Coca said Ernest Hemingway said the corrida is an art, a ballet where you demonstrate grace under pressure, when you kill truly."

"Kill is a horrid word," Dr. Forest said.

"That in the bull's death you become one with the bull."

"Bullshit." Dr. Forest took a long pull on his cigar and let out all the smoke at once, the blue cloud concealing, protecting us from the enemy. "Excuse the army language, boys, but I'm afraid your Ernest Hemingway is talking untruths. While the stadium mob cheers, a prancing sadist keeps sticking sharp arrows into that bull until the poor bull's bleeding like a soldier and then some tall, skinny, bouncing idiot dressed like a glittering clown comes out to try to kill the bleeding animal with a silver sword. It hurts, gentlemen. It hurts." Dr. Forest pulled out his shirt and showed us a scarlet, ragged scar on his right hip. "The bayonet of Johnny Reb. It hurt, boys, it hurt. He rushed me with his bayonet. I had to shoot him. I don't believe the young man was above sixteen. He seemed surprised at his sudden death. He said, "Save me." That hurt, boys, that hurt." The protective blue haze from Dr. Forest's Cremo smoke had vanished now and Dr. Forest looked out over the wild red-flowering meadows of Prettyfields. "Out of the cradle endlessly rocking." Dr. Forest paused in remembrance of other drums, other bloodied meadows scarlet in the new dawn. Touched his temple. "A cluster of dead in the early dew, Dr. Forest confided to us arranged in a row on the Packard running board. "They, lying there in the early dew in awkward angles. It was enough to drive a man crazy."

"Doctor Forest, will you drive us to the sanitarium to see Miss Coca?" I said.

"Why not?" Dr. Forest said.

"Because your Packard might fall apart," Clancy said.

"No, she's a daisy," Dr. Forest said, rummaging in the running board toolbox for another Cremo cigar. "I tell you what, boys, we'll stop at Charlie Keyes' and get a whole box of real cigars. A ten-cent cigar is a horrid word."

Going up Four Mile Hill, I asked Dr. Forest if I could shift.

"Why not?"

I had to go into low going up Four Mile Hill, but the Packard made it up okay, but just barely, jerking at the crest.

"You ought to get a Hupmobile."

"Or a Reo Speedwagon. A Stutz Bearcat."

"Or a horse."

Going down Four Mile Hill I asked Dr. Forest what would be a good present to get Miss Coca at Charlie Keyes'. "Chanel No. 5—shift, you're still in low. No, Charlie Keyes wouldn't carry that. What about a mink coat? Put her in high. I tell you, something like Elizabeth Barrett Browning's *Sonnets from the Portuguese*. I bet she'd like that."

At Charlie Keyes' there was nothing but "True Confessions," "True Romances," "True West," *Tarzan, Tarzan of the Apes* and *The Return of Tarzan.*

"Mister Keyes, you wouldn't happen to have Elizabeth Barrett Browning's *Sonnets from the Portuguese?*"

"I don't think so, son. You wouldn't be one of the boys who stole my cider off the front porch?"

"I don't think so, Mister Keyes."

"Well, somebody did. I'm fresh out of Cremos," he told Dr. Forest.

"Good. Then give me a real cigar."

"Mister Keyes, do you have a Chanel No. 5?"

"No, son, and I don't have a mink coat either. What about some Mexican stogies?" he told Dr. Forest. "Ten for a dollar."

At ten for a dollar we can't lose," Dr. Forest said, dropping them into his hat.

"I'll take some teardrop Hershey kisses, a Love Nest and some Necco hearts and flowers," I said.

Charlie Keyes made a neat package of the candies. "For your sweetheart?" he said.

"Kind of. Yes."

"Don't steal any more of my cider."

Outside, Dr. Forest put his stethoscope to the hood of the Packard. "There's nothing wrong with Packy that an affair with a Stutz Bearcat wouldn't cure. The Overbrook Sanitarium or bust."

Between Millington and Basking Ridge, Dr. Forest said, "Drop her in high, Billy. You know, I think you got a crackerjack present."

"I didn't get any Crackerjacks."

"I know. You got kisses, a Love Nest, and what else?"

"Necco Wafers hearts and flowers."

"Well, that's crackerjack. She'll like that, Billy."

At the Somerset County mental hospital we all trooped

through the endless maze of hard white sanitary and penal tunnels to the receptionist at the grand entrance.

"You can't go in."

"I'm a doctor. Elizabeth Mary Coca is my patient."

"She's not your patient, Doctor Forest. She's under the care of a psychiatrist. I'm very sorry, Doctor Forest."

Dr. Forest was in bad repute with the medical profession in Somerset County. He was getting much too old for competence. Another charge was he seldom recommended surgery. He never pulled any tonsils. Said it was a waste of money. Never did a hysterectomy. Said it was a waste of women. He called it fooling around with a woman's private parts to make a fortune. But worst of all, he wrote a letter published in the *Newark Evening News* about "the crooks in my profession I have known." He was thrown out of the A.M.A., the American Medical Association. "To hell with them," Dr. Forest said. "Wait till they start another war and want me to serve."

"I'm sorry, Doctor Forest." The receptionist continued to patronize our friend. I don't think friend is the word. We loved Dr. Forest.

"Everybody loves me," Dr. Forest said, "but the very old get very little consideration." But right now he said to the receptionist, "Try and stop me. I got a small army here and if cornered we'll fight."

The receptionist didn't try to stop us. She didn't even call up her starched white battalions. She just watched us attack down the corridor through her pince-nez.

I gave Miss Coca the present.

She just stared at us quietly.

"Well," she said, "what do we have here, *Finnegan's Wake*? Everyone from the creative writing class. I'm surprised they let you in, Doctor Forest."

"We had to fight our way in," Dr. Forest said. "They forgot to lay minefields and they forgot to string barbed wire. They're running a lousy prison. Are they treating you okay?"

"Not too bad. They let me take a call from Zelda, Scott's wife. She's having problems too."

"I don't like to hear that," Dr. Forest said.

"Well, it's very difficult being married to a writer."

"Have you heard from Thomas Wolfe?" I said.

"Not a word."

"I looked all over for a copy of Elizabeth Barrett Browning's *Sonnets from the Portuguese*," I said. "No luck."

"I prefer this," she said, opening the candies and taking out a silver kiss. "I like the symbolism. Still, I like Joyce's line," Miss Coca said. "No symbols where no cymbals intended."

Now the white-starched battalion arrived and threw us out.

Outside, getting into the Packard, Dr. Forest dropped the Mexican stogies into the running board toolbox and said, "I didn't put up a fight in there because I felt it was time to withdraw from our position. It wasn't that they had us outflanked or outgunned. It was that Elizabeth Mary was tired and under heavy sedation. We'll be back. Are you kids game?"

We were all game.

Dr. Forest looked up at the cloud-ragged sky. "'Youth, large, lusty, loving—youth full of grace, force, fascination. Do you know that Old Age may come after you with equal grace, force, fascination?'" Dr. Forest recovered himself and looked down at us. "You're all good soldiers."

*   *   *

The creative writing class at Prettyfields was never the same again after Miss Coca. Nothing seemed to work anymore. A man named something like Master Brown, I think, took it over. Anyway, he taught from novels like *Ivanhoe* and other "classics" that Miss Coca called "born dead." I went to see Miss Coca twice more before she went under. The last time, I managed to get hold of a copy of Elizabeth Barrett Browning's *Sonnets from the Portuguese* in Bernardsville and brought it to Miss Coca, but she did not recognize me. But the time before that, she said as I left, "Try to keep up with your oral history of Prettyfields, William. Or is it the world? The world's not a very pretty place, is it, William?"

Outside and in the open yellow straight-eight Packard again and accomplishing the last black asphalt hill again before the flat green of Prettyfields again, Dr. Forest mused to no one and everyone again in a kind of soft, secret sharing with us of his friend, his mentor, his Camden, New Jersey, camerado in celestial sphere music, "And now what do you see, Walt Whitman? I see the battlefields of the earth and now grass grows upon them and blossoms and wheat. I see Elizabeth Mary, unrequited, dying, well-beloved, saying to the people, do not weep for me, this is not my true country. I have lived banished from my true country. I now go back there, I return to the celestial sphere where everyone goes in his turn."

"Doctor Forest?"

No answer. Only the shriek noises of the wind and the burn

from the sunshot air in a yellow open straight-eight running-fast touring Packard.

"Doctor Forest?"

"Yes, son?"

"Do you believe that in the dark night of the soul it is always three o'clock in the morning?"

"But I also believe—" Dr. Forest said, holding tight to the wooden steering wheel, "but I also believe that in the bright noon of the soul it is always—"

"Always what?"

"A great time to live," Dr. Forest said.

WHEN WE HEARD on the radio from Orson Welles that men from Mars had landed in the Watchung Mountains not far from Prettyfields, the first thought was how to make some money out of the Columbia Broadcasting System's men from Mars.

"Charge them for landing rights."

"Tell the Martians how to get to Lost Wages, Nevada."

"Las Vegas?"

"Yes."

"Sell them a good used car."

All these things occurred to us because we didn't believe a word of Orson Welles' radio play about the invasion from Mars. We noticed that the first thought of the neighbor farm people was to kill the Martians. They didn't think to get out the welcome wagon and make the newcomers happy on our planet, knowing the Martians must be tired after a long trip. The second thought our neighbors had after killing the Martians was to destroy Mars with intergalactic ballistic missiles.

The reason that individual states like New Jersey, Rhode Island, New York and Connecticut did not go it alone but united with other states to form the United States is because states like zNew

Jersey could not afford a war to defend their honor. War without a billion-dollar budget would go out of style. Our Political Science teacher Abraham Popitz preached this to us with fervor, with elan, with jumping up and down. The secret of getting all the money you want to make war is to change the name of our War Department to the Defense Department. Then we could kill off everyone else in the universe and we could live happily ever after. I don't know why Popitz wasn't fired from Prettyfields, because he also believed that the United States of America was founded by our founding fathers on this continent fourscore and eighty years ago dedicated to the proposition of making a decent profit, continuing to enslave the blacks and not permitting women the vote. When we ran into Popitz' room and told him the Martians had landed, he said, "Good. Now we can get a little work done around here."

"Aren't you curious to see what men from Mars look like?"

"I assume, gentlemen, they look like Martians. They probably have an antenna coming out of their heads and they are green." We could tell Popitz didn't believe Orson Welles either.

"What is it," Popitz said, "that makes us want to believe that which is not true? Creatures from outer space are more popular than we poor creatures in space."

Popitz was our philosophy mentor too. When in class, he told us, "Cogito, ergo sum—I think, therefore I am," Raymond Hall came back with "Erecto, ergo sum—I get an erection, therefore I am." And Popitz cut if off with, "Shut up. I should never have left Russia."

Abraham Popitz had belonged to a splinter Trotskyite group in Liberty Corner of eleven members dedicated to overthrowing the

United States government by force of talk. When Popitz quit the party to work on the Roosevelt-Garner campaign, the chairman of the Liberty Corner Trotskyite Central Committee grabbed the deserter by his lapels and shouted, "Very well, Comrad Popitz, we will seize power without you."

But right now, Popitz refused to get out of bed to cope with the invaders from Mars.

We got back to the Atwater-Kent radio and Orson Welles in the recreation room. Orson Welles said that our section of New Jersey was done for, that there was very little hope, that no one in our Somerset Country would get out alive. Morris County maybe, Essex County possibly, but Somerset County, the American Army Chief of Staff said, was already down the drain. Orson Welles wanted us not to give any aid or comfort to the enemy. Welles wanted us to hide in our vegetable cellars and if possible crawl underneath the cold potatoes as a possible defense against the Martian ray guns. To soak handkerchiefs and cover our noses against a Martian poison gas attack.

"If captured, to tell them nothing but our name, rank and serial number," Tommy Peacock said.

"Why don't we warn the natives?" Raymond Hall said.

"You mean get a horse and spread the alarm through every Middlesex village and farm? The Martians are coming!"

"Prettyfields only has four horses."

"It only takes one horse to spread the alarm through every Middlesex village and farm. The Martians are coming!"

But we used all four horses, the better to spread the alarm. The horses' names were Sally, Brett, Norwood and John and they all had brands. We did not brand horses in New Jersey, so the brands meant the horses were from the wild, wild west, from near Albuquerque, New Mexico where our Bishop Tynan had a friend who raised horses or "whose father was a horse thief."

I rode Sally. Brett, Norwood and John were ridden by Tommy Peacock, Howard Tordiff and Raymond Hall. We were selected to spread the alarm about the Martian invasion because we were the only ones who were not bucked off. The only ones from the gang who slept in Trinity Hall who had staying power.

"We've got moxie," Tommy Peacock said.

The first people to be alerted to the threat to our fragile planet were the Bonapartes, a farm family that raised Polish pigs and fat children whom Popitz called "ethnics."

Luigi Bonaparte, the leader of the clan, was already on horse, carrying a shotgun and reconnoitering the rough terrain of birches and dogwood between the lower hill he had planted in winter wheat and his undrainable swamp.

"Any luck, Mister Bonaparte?"

"I think I gotta two of them."

"Only two?"

"He sure sounds like an ethnic," Raymond Hall said.

"Maybe I don'ta got nothing. It wasa early, only halfa light. Two of somathing ran into thosa cattails in the swampa and I letta them have it. I don'ta wanna getta into the swampa where they coulda corner me."

"You sure must be an ethnic."

"Shut up, Hall," I said. "Mister Bonaparte, you sure you didn't see a couple of deer?"

"No, they were from Mars-a."

"How did you know?"

"I tella you boys, I know a Martian when I see-a one. No, I don'ta. But why take a chansa?"

"Why indeed?"

"Shoota to kill."

"Yes, indeed."

"If heesa deer, then no harma is done."

"No harm at all. Then you believed Orson Welles, Mister Bonaparte, when he said the Martians are coming?"

"No, he said-a the Martians are-a here."

"That's right," Howard Tordiff said. "Orson Welles said the Martians had arrived shooting from the hip."

"And you believed that, Mister Bonaparte?"

"No, I no believa nothing."

"Are you speaking for all the ethnics?"

"Shut up, Howee," I said. "Then why, Mister Bonaparte, if you don't believe anything you hear on the radio, why did you shoot into the cattails?"

"I am because I shoot," Raymond Hall said.

"Please let Mister Bonaparte answer."

"Whata did he say?" Mister Bonaparte said.

"He said you are because you shoot."

We left Mr. Bonaparte at the bottom of his rye hill, watching into the tall brown cattails with his gun cocked, waiting for some movement at which to shoot.

If we are because we shoot, then the hills and dales of Prettyfields are because of the Ice Age when the great cold glaciers slid over them and went bumpity-bump. The patch forests of Prettyfields with a mixture of all the temperate trees are because the cunning Indian needed a forest to lurk.

"What does it mean, the cunning Indian needed a forest to lurk?"

I let this pass and watched over at the Watchung Mountains where according to Orson Welles the Mars people were dropping to our earth like flies.

Next we met a bunch of rifle-carrying vigilantes stopped on the Four Mile Hill in a Ford V8 wire-wheel coupe of the kind John Dillinger, Bonnie and Clyde, and Pennsylvania school teachers drove. They appeared like city people from Morristown in store-bought bright red plaid hunting outfits who flashed here outside of Prettyfields each hunting season to get drunk and shoot at things that moved.

"Any luck?" we said.

"We saw a squad of Martians the south side of Tupper's place, but they gave us the slip before we got a shot in." The hunters were sitting on the running board of the V8, passing a bottle. A man alone in the rumble seat was not drinking.

"You sure they were Martians?" we said.

"As sure as I'm sitting here."

"What did they look like?"

"Martians."

"What do Martians look like?"

"Actually, we really didn't have a good look."

"If we did, we would have got a shot in," another said.

"I sure would like to see a man from Mars before I die," Howard Tordiff said.

"If you parade around on that horse much longer in full sight of the enemy, I think maybe you'll die quick."

"Yes," the rumble seat said. "You'd do better without that tall profile. Why don't you get off and lead your horses—lower your silhouette?"

"Because," I said, "we can see better up here."

"Have you seen anything?"

"Not yet," I said.

"If you see something, holler."

"We really don't believe there are any Martians out there."

"What do you think it is, then?"

"What do we think *what* is?"

"The people landing in the mountains."

"We don't know."

"Then why take a chance?" The man on the end of the V8 running board took a sip from a bottle of Sunnybrook bourbon and thought about it. "Why risk your life? If we can get them before they get a chance to dig in, we'll make it through O.K."

"Supposing," the man in the middle of the running board said, "the whole thing is a hoax?"

"Then what about those Martians we saw shooting hell for leather south of Tupper's place?"

"I didn't see them."

"Well, the rest of us did."

Silence, with only the hiss of steam from the V8 radiator.

"You need water."

"Yes, we do, son. Where can we get it?"

"Charlie Keyes'."

"Where's that?"

"Two miles north."

"Does Charlie Keyes carry liquor?"

"Yes."

"We'd appreciate it if you'd ride back and get us a pail of water and a fifth of Sunnybrook while you're at it. Here's five," he said, standing up and getting out his wallet. "You can keep the change."

"The boys are too young to buy liquor," the rumble seat said. "Why don't we just scout around on foot until the engine cools off."

I took the five while they argued.

"Because I don't think we should go too far from the car in enemy territory."

"Supposing," Tommy Peacock said, "they are not the enemy. Supposing they have arrived to bring us tidings of great joy. For example, that unto your world a Savior has arrived saying everything is not relative."

"Say that again?"

"A Savior has arrived—nothing is relative."

"How much have we had to drink? Am I hearing things?"

"Young man, you better give me my fiver back."

But we had already swung our horses, and took off over Oat Hill through the oats that were already greening.

"What do you mean, Tommy Peacock, 'For example, unto your world a Savior has arrived with tidings of great joy—everything is not relative, nothing is relative'?"

Tommy Peacock did not answer, and me thinking, riding in the silence, it's because Peacock has more imagination than Orson Welles and the other Wells—H.G. Wells—who wrote *The War of the Worlds* or something like that that Miss E. Mary Coca, our creative writing teacher, was crazy about. It's not enough to have another invasion from another planet—all that old stuff of the two Wells and Buck Rogers—but you have to give the story style and not repeat a comic strip of violence as adults will and Tommy Peacock will not. Instead of announcing nothing is relative, why not have someone from outer space save us from the Hoovers, J. Edgar and Herbert, and all those that Popitz is angry with?

"If Bill here," Howard Tordiff said, pointing at me, "if Bill had his wire recorder along, he would not only be able to take down the oral history of the world that he says he's working on, but the oral history of other planets too. If we have luck enough to contact the men from Mars."

"I've got the wire recorder with me," I said.

"Good. Now all we have to do is find the men from Mars."

"They're probably all down at Charlie Keyes' eating Mars bars."

"In all probability Martians don't exist," I said.

"Why not?"

"Because Mars has been studied since Copernicus first looked, and as our Polly Platt, Psychology I—"

"What does Polly Platt know. What does any woman know?"

"Polly Platt was the first to take off and look for the Martians. What does any woman know? Polly Platt knows."

"Enough to know Mars is much too hot for life as we know it."

"Or even as we don't know it?"

"Probably."

"Indubitably."

"That too."

"Funny you should bring that up, Crip. Here's a man from Mars now."

"Where?"

We stopped our horses. "Where?"

"Over there beneath that far chestnut tree."

"I don't see him."

"There."

"I see him now."

"Me too."

"What do we say?"

Ask him if anything at all is relative. There must be something."

"Why don't we," I said, "just ride by him casually, pretending that this is an everyday occurrence, that his bunch is not the first to land on earth despite what he may have been told."

"Have you got your wire recorder turned on?"

"Yes."

"Then let's go."

"Don't look."

"Yes, nobody look."

Tommy Peacock rode at the end of the file. I was next with the wire recorder turned on "Interview," and Howard Tordiff and Raymond Hall brought up the rear. Raymond Hall said in a loud voice, "I wish I'd brought my Brownie camera."

"Quiet," I said back, hushed. "I want the stranger to be the first voice to appear on the recording."

We got by on the first pass without incident. We were careful to not appear aggressive. We of course carried no weapons. We were careful, too, to smile. "That was easy."

We had ridden a safe distance beyond the chestnut tree and could talk.

"Too easy."

"What did he look like?"

"I don't know."

"I don't know either."

"We weren't supposed to look."

"That's right."

"This time we'll look."

"You mean we'll try it again?"

"Yes."

"This time we'll look."

"But not stare."

"Yes, don't stare."

This time I went first so I could have a good look without staring and so I could pick his voice up on the recorder without the background noise of the clatter of the horses' hooves or loud boom of a horse fart which would ruin the sound effects. On we came, on we came. I tried not to stare, just to kind of see the visitor out of the side of my eye. Again we won, again we got right past him without being zapped or disintegrated. Certainly if there was an invasion from Mars, the message from outer space must be more like what Tommy Peacock said—nothing is relative—than what Orson Welles said—everyone is shooting to kill.

"What did the visitor look like?"

Again we were in safe talking distance.

"Kind of short."

"I thought kind of tall."

"For a Martian?"

"Yes."

"I thought he looked kind of depressed."

"We disappointed him?"

"Yes."

"He expected an antenna to come out of our heads?"

"Yes."

"He expected us to be green?"

"Yes."

"Well, we could tell him we're sorry about that."

"Yes."

"You know who he reminds me of more than anything?"

"Who?"

"Polly Platt."

"Me too."

"He had those curved brown lashes and the same long blonde hair."

"Down to the ass?"

"Yes."

"Boys." The man from Mars waved. "Boys, you rode by twice without speaking."

"Have you got your wire recorder turned on, Bill?"

"It's Polly Platt," I said.

And it was too. It kind of shows you what you see when you don't see. That a true believer will see things that don't exist without lying. That caught up in the hysteria of our time, you see things you don't see.

"Not entirely, Billy." Polly Platt walked beside us as we walked our horses back to Prettyfields away from the war of the worlds and the invasion from Mars. "Not entirely, Billy. We see things that don't exist—invading Martians, flying saucers—because what does exist—a world-wide Depression, Adolph Hitler, the absence of God—are all too much."

"Too much?"

"Yes."

"God's taking His vacation?"

"Yes. You got that thing turned on?"

"Yes."

"Well, turn it off."

"O.K."

"Don't waste your wire, Billy, till I can sum up the lesson."

"Yes."

But Polly Platt never did, that is, she never summed up the meaning of life on this planet, or if she did, she forgot to tell me to turn the recorder on. So we had to let the invasion from Mars go without a summing up. Unless it was that the real world—the continuing Depression, God's vacation, the rise of Hitler—was too much. So we needed to invent men from Mars.

"I like my summing up better," Tommy Peacock said. "Hark and behold, we bring you tidings of great joy. Unto your world a Savior has arrived announcing all is not relative, nothing is relative."

"Which calls for great shooting throughout the land."

One thing more happened to make Orson Welles' incredible incident more incredible. Someone shot at us just before we got to Prettyfields. They missed. It could have been the four drunken hunters from Morristown in the Ford V8 getting rid of their ammunition. It could not have been the Martians. Despite Orson Welles, we know now the men from Mars never showed up.

"If they had," Miss Polly Platt said, "I believe they would have brought no guns. I believe the universe is kind. Of course," she said, "with the exception of our part of it."

When we got safe within the bounds of Prettyfields, Howard Tordiff turned to the direction the shooting had come from and baited the hunters on our small and paranoid planet, "We welcome you to earth with tidings of great joy. We shoot, therefore we are."

"I get an erection, therefore I am," Raymond Hall said. "Shut up," Abraham Popitz said. "I should never have left Russia. Get out of here. Get out!"

But the boys of Prettyfields got in the last shot. Tommy Peacock leaned over and whispered into Abraham Popitz' ear, "Very well, Comrade Popitz, we will seize power without you."

III

Before the last big green rolling swale at the river called the Blue, there is a motte of wild forest that remains as virgin as it was before the white man came. We never much went into that forest. There was something wrong there. We never figured out what it was.

But what bemused Abraham Popitz our Political Science teacher as he looked from the classroom window out to the edge of the secret forest was that Dwight D. Eisenhower and Douglas MacArthur would never be able to run for political office. Their heroic pictures had just appeared on the front page of the "Newark Evening News," dressed in impeccable pinks, Sam Browne belts and leather boots that shone like the North Star. Eisenhower and MacArthur were the absolutely perfect picture of the modern major generals at the head of their battle groups, sending George Patton to spearhead the drive with four battalions of infantry and four troops of prancing cavalry armed with whippet tanks, machine guns, hand grenades and tear gas against the hungry and forgotten American veterans of World War I camped at the Anacostia flats outside Washington—come to lobby for a veterans' bonus. It was clear as a day in May that although the veterans were not Bolsheviks, they were obviously led or misled by people of a foreign nature, anarchists and such like. Pinkos. As good luck would have it, Calvin Coolidge who was not yet formally dead allowed to the press that the stern-visaged General Douglas MacArthur and his dashing aide-de-camp, young smiling Ike, may very well have saved the country. And let's not forget George S. Patton who led the charge. These gentlemen did what they had to do to perhaps save our country from a fate worse than Franklin D. Roosevelt.

"Save from what did you say?"

"Calvin Coolidge did not ever respond to silly questions. It was obvious to any red-blooded American that the problem was you cannot run a country with anarchy. And oh, remember, children of love, you cannot lobby in Washington without a proper suit, without a roll of green bills, without a high, wide, white celluloid collar to hide behind."

"But you're biased, Mister Popitz."

"No."

"Why did you start your talk by saying Eisenhower and MacArthur, after winning the battle against unarmed American vets, could never get elected to dogcatcher?"

"Did I say that?"

"Yes."

"I can maybe see General MacArthur getting elected to something, but I can't see Major Eisenhower getting elected to anything, can you?"

We were not only interested, we were concerned at Prettyfields as the war moved north, because the retreating American Expeditionary Force that had made the world safe for democracy, licked Kaiser bill, stopped the Hun from raping the nuns in neutral Belgium, protested the shooting of Mata Hari by the "Frogs," and had the triumphal tickertape welcoming up Broadway, was not a defeated, hungry mob running from the guns of their own. Their own that had sent them over there, over there, oh the Yanks are coming, the Yanks are coming, and we won't come back till it's over over there. Till it's over over here, over here, over here . . .

According to the "Millington Daily Progress," remnants of the routed American Army might arrive at Liberty Corner five miles from Prettyfields that morning, but they never showed by noon. The night before, the "Newark Evening News" had said the Americans were trying to make their way to Johnstown, Pennsylvania where the mayor, Eddie McCloskey, had said he would bed them down and give them rations. But the "Millington Daily Progress" reprinted an editorial from the "Johnstown Tribune":

"Johnstown faces a crisis. It must prepare to protect itself from the Bonus Army concentrating here at the invitation of Mayor Eddie McCloskey . . ."

In any group of the size of the Bonus Army, made up of men gathered from all parts of the country, without discipline, without effective leadership in a crisis, without any attempt on the part of those leaders to check up the previous records of the individuals who compose it, there is certain to be a mixture of undesirables—thieves, plug-uglies, degenerates . . . The community must protect itself from the criminal fringe of the invaders.

Booster clubs, community organizations of every sort, volunteer organizations if no sectional group is available, should get together in extraordinary sessions and organize to protect property, women and possibly life.

"It is no time for halfway measures . . ."

That afternoon we skipped José Jesus de la Cruz's Latin class and Dr. Van Dee's Greek and other dead, meaningless and foreign wastes of time about Cicero and Caesar, about wars lost in unremembered places long dead, long forgotten except by Mr. José Jesus de la Cruz and Dr. Van Dee. Escaped the Peloponesian Wars and "all Gaul is divided into three parts" and instead we reconnoitered along our own Blue River, hoping to pick up retreating American stragglers trying to make their way over to the Pennsylvania Turnpike before they were cut off by George Patton's 1st Cav.

"Boys!"

"Yes, Sir?"

"You don't have to 'Sir' me."

We had run into the retreating vets under the Blue River bridge where the highway crosses near Bonaparte's farm. There were about ten of the defeated ex-heroes and they all needed a shave. They needed decent clothes too, and something to eat.

"Where are we?"

"New Jersey," I said.

"We know that, but whereabouts?"

"Between Liberty Corner and Millington."

"That doesn't mean anything to us."

"Where are you people from?"

"I'm from Butler, Pennsylvania."

"Where's that?"

"Between Kittanning and New Castle."

"That doesn't mean anything to us."

"We got dumped here over a county line. The cops want to keep us moving."

"Is the army, is George Patton still chasing you?"

"Old Blood and Guts?"

"Is that what you call him?"

"Yes. No, his army just beat our army in Washington. They never followed up."

"They just depend on the State Police to keep us moving," another said. "How many were you in the beginning?"

"Fifteen thousand."

"And now?"

"We don't know. They got us scattered all over from hell to breakfast."

"But you're trying to get to Johnstown to regroup?"

"How did you know that?"

"The newspaper, the radio."

"What have you got there?"

"This is a gadget," I said, "that records what we're saying."

"I'll be damned."

"I'll be damned."

"Do you want to say something?"

"No. Do you want to say something, Mike?" he said to another.

"No, Hank. How about you, Tom?"

"No."

"Does anybody want to say anything?"

None of the retreating soldiers wanted to say anything.

"You were all doing great," our Raymond Hall said, "until you realized you were being recorded."

"Then you became self-conscious," I said. "Do you want me to turn this thing off?"

"I guess you better."

"No," someone said from the shadow of the bridge abutment. "I got something to say into that thing." He looked bad. Kind of too much gray in his face skin behind a thick black beard. His eyes were red-shot and he coughed into his big hands. "Where's the mike?"

"Right here."

"Fuck the United States."

"You want to add something to that?" I said.

He coughed again. "No."

"Anything at all?"

"I got a dose of phosgene gas in the Meuse-Argonne from the Krauts." He coughed.

"Keep talking, Harry," someone said.

"I came back to the states—"

"Keep going, Harry."

"And the sons of bitches gassed me again right outside the Capitol."

"Anacostia flats, Harry."

"They came at us with tanks and drawn sabers."

"They burnt our tents and huts down," someone said, "and the cavalry chased us on horseback with drawn sabers."

"I saw a guy lose an ear."

"After they scattered us, we wandered around looking for our buddies."

"Some of us our families."

"Nothing to eat or drink, the tear gas burning the hell out of our eyes."

"They blocked the bridge so we couldn't escape into Virginia."

"They finally let us into Maryland, but told us to keep moving."

The man called Harry had stopped his coughing. "I got something more to say."

"Go ahead," I said.

"I threw my war medals into the river what's-its-name."

"The Blue?"

"That's where I threw them," he said, and the man called Harry started coughing again. "When's the last time you men had anything to eat?" our Little Clancy wanted to know.

"God knows."

"Well, I got an idea," Clancy said.

"I got something more to say," the man who coughed said.

"Go ahead," I said.

"Is that thing running?"

"Yes."

The man who coughed started to say something into the machine and then he began coughing again.

"You better call it quits, Harry," the man called Mike who seemed to be in charge said.

"Yes, you can tell it to the reporters in Johnston."

"If we ever get to Johnstown."

"We'll get to Johnstown if we stick together."

Harry stopped coughing now and asked if I was ready, if he could go ahead and talk.

"Go ahead."

"This country has declared war on itself."

"You tell 'em, Harry."

"And lost."

"That's right, Harry."

"I'm not Harry anymore," Harry said. "I left Harry or whoever I was back there at the Anacostia flats or wherever we were when our own army fired at us. I don't know who the hell I am now." Harry gave a quick cough before he started again. But first Harry placed his busted hat over his heart. "I pledge allegiance to the flag," Harry said, "and to the Republic for which it stands, one nation indivisible with liberty and justice for all. What's that mean now?"

"You tell 'em, Harry."

Harry wanted to say something more into the microphone, but he started coughing again. "You better call it quits, Harry," a vet said.

"When's the last time you people had anything to eat?" our Little Clancy wanted to know again.

"God knows."

"Well, I got an idea."

"So you said. What is it?"

"Why don't we go up to Bonaparte's crabapple and peach orchard and fill up?"

"We couldn't do that," their leader Mike said.

"No, we're not a bunch of thieves," another said.

"It's not stealing," Little Clancy said. "Since the Depression, nobody can buy nothing. The apples and the peaches rot on the trees. You might say you're doing Mister Bonaparte a favor."

"You sure?"

"Sure I'm sure."

"All right," the man called Hank said. "Let's get moving to the hill, gentlemen."

In the hobgoblin shifting and cool shadowing of the peach trees you could see better the faces of those who had been the American Expeditionary Force that had gone eager to France and shot at vague phantom figures in different helmets and got shelled, gassed and bayoneted right back. At home now, no one wanted to hear about that war. War is sad. So the soldiers got together, joined by a common defeat, not to talk about the war but to be with the silent who understood. There were very few jobs. No work. A soldiers' bonus had been promised. They wanted it now. Someone in Washington had said that to postpone relief would be better in the long run and someone answered, "Yes, Senator, but people don't eat in the long run. They eat every day."

"This could mean," someone from the speckled shade said, "this could be the start of a revolution."

"No, it takes money to start a revolution."

"Funny thing," someone said. "You can always raise billions for bombs to start a war, but after it's over not a nickel to pay for it."

"Yes," another said. "Let's sit around here all day feeling sorry for ourselves."

"Jesus, Tom, it was your idea to march on Washington."

"Was it? I thought it was everybody's idea."

"Maybe."

"We should have realized it would turn out to be another Coxey's Army.

"What was Coxey s Army?"

"That's when another bunch of sorry bastards like ourselves marched on Washington to get work and got their asses whipped."

"Yeah."

"You can't beat the system."

"Who said you could?"

"You can never beat it."

"Lo, the poor vet," another soldier said.

"It's not funny."

"Who said it was funny?"

"You know what I think is funny?"

"What?"

"I think it's funny that the war that started in France ended right here under a peach tree in—where did you say we were?"

"New Jersey," our Raymond Hall said.

"We know that. Whereabouts in New Jersey?"

"Liberty Corner."

"The war ended in Liberty Corner, New Jersey. I think that's funny." The man coughed.

"Well," a shadow said, "I don't understand your sense of humor, Harry."

"I still think it's funny," Harry said, and then he went into a spell of coughing that I thought would never stop. The coughing never did quite stop, but became low-keyed and muffled by Harry's big hands. Then there was a silence and a gun went off and there was a rain of small shot hitting into the overhead branches like shrapnel. All the soldiers hit the deck. None of them moved to reveal their position. They all seemed dead.

"That was Mister Bonaparte," our Big Clancy said. "But he never aimed this close to us before. He usually fires straight in the air with the first shot to warn us to stop stealing his peaches. He must have learned you people are in the area. Let's all make a run for the bridge."

Mike, who was their leader, gave an arm signal to his outfit and without picking up any more fire we all made it down to the concealment of the bridge again. After a few minutes it got very quiet in the darkness and our position seemed safe.

"I got an idea," Little Clancy said.

"You already had one idea."

"I got another one."

"Another one?"

"A better one."

"What?"

"The airship, the Hindenburg."

"What about it?"

"It crosses Millington and Prettyfields tomorrow at four on its way to Lakehurst."

"And so?"

"When everybody's watching, we can rob the kitchen blind— enough food to get you fellas on the road again."

"We're not crooks."

"We're not crooks either," our Big Clancy said, "but we believe in redistributing the wealth."

"Firm believers?"

"Yes."

"Dedicated to that cause?"

"Kind of."

"We'll wait here for you to see how you make out."

We got up and the man called Harry had stopped his cough-ing and said, "You still got that recording machine turned on?"

"Yes."

"What in the hell are you up to?"

"What I'm attempting to do," I said, moving through the shadows, "what I'm trying to accomplish is an oral history of mankind."

"That sounds pretentious as hell."

"Oh."

"Lay off the kid, Harry."

"You sound very young," Harry said to me. "One of these days you'll see."

"See what?"

"Nothing."

"Listen," I said. "I understand that it's rough all over."

"Well, you're beginning to see," Harry said.

The next day we had a game of Knife while waiting for the Hindenburg to arrive. While Raymond Hall was trying to get the knife to stick in the ground from a standing position, Mr. Popitz, Political Science, came up and asked us if we had seen anything of the Hindenburg.

"Not yet."

"I'd like to see her crash or explode or burn," Popitz said.

"Why?"

"The Nazi swastika on the tail. Those people are advertising murder."

"Why are you gathering up rocks, Mister Popitz?"

It was not a good question, because we knew he gathered rocks to throw at the German airship every time she passed over Prettyfields on her way to her port at Lakehurst. We asked anyway to make conversation and maybe to add to my oral history of the world.

"You know why," Popitz said.

Yes, we did. As Polly Platt, Psychology I, had figured, "Even if of course he can't hit the Hindenburg, can't come within a mile of it, it still works."

"What do you mean, it works?"

"Well, the moon can't hear a wolf when the wolf bays at the moon. Yet it does the wolf a lot of good to bay at the moon."

"How do you know the moon can't hear the wolf, Miss Platt?"

"Because we know an inanimate object can't hear anything, and I refuse to discuss the occult. This is supposed to be a school, not a lunatic asylum."

"The 'Newark Evening News' prints an astrology column every day, Miss Platt."

"As somebody has already pointed out, "Polly Platt said, "Shirley Temple and Adolf Hitler were born in the same month under the same sign. I don't know how the 'Newark Evening News' copes with that contradiction, except they can blame every problem on their circulation problem. If you ask the editor of the 'News' what sign he was born under, he'd probably admit the dollar sign, but I still believe in wolves baying at the moon and Abe Popitz throwing rocks at the Hindenburg swastika because I believe in a good night's sleep, and one way to get a good night's sleep is to shoot down the Hindenburg."

"Strong stuff, Miss Platt."

"Because I'm a strong young lady, Polly Platt said. "You boys better believe it."

Now we backtracked with Mr. Popitz. "Alright, we agree. 'Why are you picking up rocks?' is not a good question. A good question is, do you agree with Miss Platt that baying at the moon and throwing rocks at the mile-high Hindenburg are identical?"

"I suppose so, yes."

"And helpful?"

"Yes, if I get my licks in, I'll sleep like a top tonight."

"Mister Popitz, here's some rocks." We tossed some rocks at his feet. "Mister Popitz, do you believe marching on Congress, petitioning Congress without a million-dollar bill in your hand and without a flag in your hat is like baying at the moon or tossing rocks at the sky-high Hindenburg?"

"You mean the bonus marchers?"

"Yes."

"I don't know."

"You want to reserve judgment?"

"Yes."

"You got your own problems."

"I didn't say that."

We got up from our game of Knife and moved toward the dining hall, leaving Mr. Popitz to shoot down the Hindenburg on his time off.

Goldy and Gilmore, assisted by Pat Patman, were Prettyfields' black chief cook and bottlewashers and the protectors of all the food in the world. Our purpose in life was to get Goldy and

Gilmore (Pat was drunk) to come out of the kitchen and watch
the Hindenburg pass over Prettyfields.

"I've seen the Hindenburg pass over Prettyfields," Gilmore
said.

"Now they got a new sign on the tail rudder."

"What it say?"

"You remember on the Hindenburg where the Nazis had the
swastika, those hooked crosses? Well, now they got an ad for car
wax. It says, MOTORISTS WISE SIMONIZE.

"Do it?"

"Yes."

"Well, me and Goldy saw that ad many times and we're not
going to get sunburnt to see it again."

I suppose that is the meaning of Horatio Alger—when you
fail, try, try again. Goldy and Gilmore played the numbers. You
gave seventy-five cents to a numbers runner for Dutch Schultz,
Legs Diamond or Kid Twist and at odds of a million to one you
won untold wealth. Gilmore was always asking us to tell him a
number that would change his luck. "They got a new
identification number on the tail of the Hindenburg."

"Let's go. Let's go see," Goldy and Gilmore said.

When we got back to where the bridge crosses the Blue near
Bonaparte's farm with all the food in the world, nobody was
home. All the heroes of the world had folded their tents and
continued their retreat into a country that nobody knew.

The next day the "Millington Daily Progress" said that the
army of veterans had been sent on their way by the New Jersey
State Troopers, that there was no longer any cause for alarm.
There was a picture of our veterans from under the bridge. They

were being herded down the road by the State Troopers in green uniforms and Boy Scout wide, flat-brimmed campaign hats. The prisoners looked prepared to tell only their name, rank and serial number. And there must have been hope that the New Jersey State Troopers would abide by the Geneva Convention and feed them before they passed the vets over the Pennsylvania line. If you held the "Millington Daily Progress" up to the light, you could make out the face of Harry, the man who threw his medals into the Blue. Harry appeared to be walking in his sleep. Like the others, he looked lost behind the enemy lines in a country where nobody spoke the language.

"But what concerns me," Mr. Popitz, Political Science, said, "is the factor of altruism. Why will you boys rob Goldy and Gilmore to pay the unfortunate? And why will you same boys when you become men ignore the dispossessed? Why the abrupt change to law and order? What happens to the thoughts of our youth? What changes the respect for a life into respect for the uniform?"

"Say that again."

"You wouldn't understand."

"Try us."

"You're too young."

"What does altruism mean?"

"Look it up."

"Did you hit the Hindenburg?"

"You know I didn't."

"Miss Rasbridge, Psychology II, says your throwing stones at the Hindenburg shows regressive behavior, a need to return to the child."

"I hope she's right, " Mr. Popitz said.

"What do you mean by that?"

"Nothing, that's all. I hope she's right. Class dismissed."

When the Blue was running low we would look through the cold, clear water for those medals. We never saw anything down there that shined like a medal should. After we gave up looking, we got to believing that maybe that soldier called Harry never did throw his medals away. Maybe he was never awarded any medals to throw away. Then one Sunday after a quick raid on Bonaparte's orchard, Howard Todiff picked up, washed on the bank, a dull bronze coin attached to a purple ribbon.

"A Purple Heart."

"I guess that means he was wounded."

"Where?"

"Over there."

"Here too?"

"It could be."

We thought about sending it to the veteran because he might have changed his mind about this country now. Maybe he got a job. Maybe his country paid off on the bonus they promised. Maybe it all ended happily ever after. But maybe not. Anyway, we didn't know where to send the medal or to whom. Someone—maybe it was Harry—said he was from Butler, Pennsylvania. But there are probably a lot of Harrys in Butler.

Getting back to Prettyfields with the Purple Heart we took the through-the-forest shortcut and it began to rain, and getting through the thick brush and the low-growing second growth was tough going. Then the rain would stop for a minute and the wind would moan through the tall, darkened trees, then the thunder would come again like sharp cracks of cannon and you stopped and waited for the world to end before you moved again. Carrying the dulled medal with the purple ribbon through the shadowed forest, you kind of got to know what it must be like to be lost and forgotten in a strange war so close to the familiar hills of home.

"I KNOW A GREAT DEAL about people because I sit around listening to them breathe."

Dr. Forest, our doctor at Prettyfields, made that profound statement. Dr. Forest knew little about medicine but a great deal about the curifying powers of love and laughter, the medicaments of compassion and humor, like some grave, penultimate or maybe final Indian still searching for the humanity in the innocent, the lost, the misbegot, the abandoned at Prettyfields, in the great human retreat, a war that had wandered someplace else. Dr. Forest would tell you to cough when he put the frozen stethoscope to your heart, then he would say, "If you take care of yourself, lay off the sex, you've got about two days to live."

"What color pills do I get, Doctor Forest?"

"The green ones."

"I had the green ones last time. The red ones."

"I'm all out of red ones," Dr. Forest said. "How about a bottle of all colors?"

Dr. Forest had a Packard and he would repeat, "Ask the man who owns one," every time the engine failed. Once he got in an accident at Liberty Corner and he leaked pills all the way to

Prettyfields. Dr. Forest had been a drummer boy in the Civil War, he was that old. He had noticed that the Sanitation Commission never got hit by a bullet, so after the war he became a doctor. He was that smart. Dr. Forest had been born and studied medicine in Camden, New Jersey, where his mother had known Walt Whitman.

"The old bastard used to come around to the back door with that basket of books and that big white beard, but I tell you, boys, there never was a better poet." And Dr. Forest would recite "When Lilacs Last in the Dooryard Bloom'd" and the tears would drop on our cold shoulders and the stethoscope would shake, and then he would stride the floor, the stethoscope swinging from his neck like the drum of the New Jersey Volunteers that once hung there, and he would talk army talk. "The old son of a bitch could write." Then he would say solemnly, "We are coming, Father Abraham, a hundred thousand strong."

"Did you work a machine gun, Doctor Forest?"

"We didn't even have a breech-loading rifle," Dr. Forest said. "We had to load the bastard from the muzzle. They had invented metal cartridges then, but they was afraid we'd use too much ammunition with a breechloader."

"But you said you was only a drummer boy, Doctor Forest."

"I was called that," Dr. Forest said, "because I was very young. Everyone who wasn't old enough to get shot at was called a drummer boy. I wasn't much older than you boys."

"Is there a chance we can get in a war as drummer boys, Doctor Forest?"

"No. They don't have them anymore," Dr. Forest said. "Now in order to get killed you'd have to lie about your age."

Dr. Forest lived in Far Hills. When he was eighty-seven years old that's how fast he drove from Far Hills to Prettyfields Academy, and when he was eighty-eight that's how fast he drove. He would hop out of the car, then reach back in as an afterthought and pull out his long legs and say, "Four minutes and twenty seconds. Averaged eighty-seven. That's how fast I made it and that's how old I am. Anyone want to fight?" And then he would toss us his cap and when we caught it he'd say, "That's a daisy. Any deaths today, Cowboy?" he would say to me. He never smiled when he called me Cowboy as the boys did. "Any boy can have a love affair with a car. Very common. A horse—" Then he would touch me. "Very uncommon."

"There are only two kinds of boys, those that die and those that don't, and who am I to fool around with nature? I'll take you like Grant took Richmond. I'll fight it out on these lines if it takes all summer. That's a daisy, boy. That's a daisy."

"How's the Packard running, Doctor Forest?"

"Ask the man who owns one. It's a daisy. Anybody alive today, Billy?" Then he would remove his Gladstone of pills from the trunk. They were heavy, but he swung them as though they were light as a drum. He carried the stethoscope in his left coat pocket, the stethoscope that had been clogged and useless for two years. Dr. Forest carried a bundle of knives in his right coat pocket. When he was going to cut you open he would spread the knives out in front of you and say, "Now which one do you want, boy?" Then he would burn the knife you had selected with a match, poise before the boil and say, "Now this is going to hurt you more than it hurts me." When we all lined up in the dispensary he would say, "Well, this was quite a defeat, but we'll give them hell tomorrow, boys." If he removed a splinter he would say, "A piece of Minnie ball." If you cut yourself with a knife it was a bad saber wound. "But we'll give them hell tomorrow," Dr. Forest said. Then he would recite something from Walt Whitman and say, "He was the best poet that Camden, New Jersey, produced at that time." Then he would line his knives up on the consulting table in a semi-circle. "Now supposing you are Grant before Petersburg. Each of these knives is a division. Now supposing you were going to attack, sweep way around here on our right flank and roll up the Confederate rear. Now, how do one of these divisions, way over here, get in position for the attack over here on the right?"

"If you were going to use one division," Howie Tordiff said, "you have each division move one position to the right."

"Not Grant," Dr. Forest said. "You take one division out of the line"—he picked up a knife—"from here on the left flank and you move it back of the other divisions over here in position for your attack. This way you move only one division and your line is not disturbed. You know, it's not true about General Grant drinking to excess."

"It isn't?"

"No," Dr. Forest said. "He only drank when it was available. That was the joke he told on the lines." Dr. Forest said. "I saw General Grant once. He had come out of his tent to put on his pants in the early morning and take a leak. He must have slept with his cigar in his mouth because that's the way he came out of the tent wrestling with those pants, and he spoke to me."

"What did he say?"

"Hello, boy," Dr. Forest said. "He just had time to say, 'Hello, boy,' and then he got his pants on and went back into the tent. I saw the back of Abraham Lincoln once, too. The New Jersey Volunteers marched through Washington on their way to the Potomac. 'We are coming, Father Abraham, a hundred thousand strong!' It was dark and there were just those torches to see by. He was walking away across the White House lawn and I saw his back."

"How did you know it was Lincoln?"

"You couldn't mistake him," Dr. Forest said. "There was never another. He was walking away and then he stopped and took something out of his hat. He must have piled a whole office in that hat. Then he put his hat back and walked on again till he was out of the light of the torches. There was no mistaking him. Then the New Jersey Volunteers went on to the Potomac to fight under General McClellan, or not to fight."

"How was General McClellan?"

"Oh, he was a son of a bitch," Dr. Forest said. "How is your head today?"

"Worse."

"Then you better try some of those purple pills," Dr. Forest said.

But we always got better and nobody died, so I guess Dr. Forest was right when he said it takes a cannon to kill a Union boy.

"What kind of a commander is Master Eaton?" Dr. Forest said, referring to the coach of Prettyfields, rolling a bandage on his finger and looking at us with those blue slit Civil War eyes, coldly as though assessing a rout at Shiloh.

"Chief Eaton's no good," Charlie Peacock said. "He tries to understand us."

"Never try to understand boys," Dr. forest said. "Certain defeat. You can lead them, bully them, command them, but you can never understand them. Never try to understand boys. That's what happened at Bull Run."

"That's what we like about you, Doctor Forest," Pete Nelson said. "You talk to us like we was human beans."

"Have one of these big red pills," Dr. Forest said, picking a pill up and tossing it, and when Pete Nelson caught it Dr. Forest said, "That's a daisy, a perfect daisy, Peter Nelson."

"When we grow up can we fight with you, Doctor Forest?"

"For me or against me?"

"With you," Howie Tordiff said.

"I'm too old," Dr. Forest said, ruminating, unrolling the bandage again. "Although if Master Eaton is the best they can do—" Then he took one of his own pills, rolled it around on his tongue, smacked his lips and said, "Not bad. You know, it wouldn't take too much to improve on the commanders they send into the line now. It wouldn't take much," he said, gathering up his knives. "Even an old lollapaloosa like me."

"Do you want us to help you carry your junk out to the Packard, Doctor Forest?"

"That'll be the day," Dr. Forest said. "That will be the day."

"I didn't get any yellow pills, Doctor Forest."

"Neither did I," Dr. Forest said. "I only got one white one," and he swung out with all that stuff to the Packard like he was not only carrying all the Union drums but most of the artillery too.

America's Sweetheart and Baby Face Nelson got in the front

seat first. The rest of us piled in the back. We usually rode part of the way to Far Hills with Dr. Forest. Once we went all the way.

"We'll see those rich bastards' houses," Dr. Forest said. "They call them estates. Stockbrokers. The first fire fight, the first artillery shells, and they've had it. The first time the market drops fifty points they start committing suicide. From the roof of their stables on to the tennis court. Nobody can panic like the rich. Young men, never try to understand the rich either."

"Yes, Sir."

"Who's going to crank?"

We were all piled in the car, so many of us we made a pyramid.

"Who's going to get out and crank?" Dr. Forest repeated.

"I thought you had an electric starter."

"It's busted," Dr. Forest said. "Ask the man who owns one."

"We'll all get out and push," Charlie Peacock said. "If somebody cranks, somebody's likely to bust their arm and we'll need a real doctor."

"That's true," Dr. Forest said. "Everybody get out and push."

We got it started by pushing it and we all piled back on.

"How far are you people going?" Dr. Forest said. "Are you going as far as the rich people's houses?"

"Maybe."

"They never own their houses," Dr. Forest said. "Nobody owns them. They don't even own the tennis courts they commit suicide on. Are you boys going to vote for Herbert Hoover?"

"We're too young. Anyway, Hoover already lost the election."

"Markowitz," Dr. Forest said to Eddie without letting go of the wheel, "I understand your father fought in the Revolutionary War. Well, of course you are too young for that."

"It was my great-great grandfather. Very great."

"So none of you boys are going to vote for Herbert," Dr. Forest said, studying the road over the big wooden wheel, down the long straight-eight hood. "Well, everybody in Far Hills, all the rich, were going to vote for Herbert Hoover before they committed suicide. Who will vote for Herbert Hoover now?" And then abruptly changing the subject, Dr. Forest said, "Did I ever tell you boys about my life in the South after the Civil War?"

"No, Sir."

"Well, the New Jersey Volunteers did occupation duty in Meridian, Mississippi, when the war was over. Cotton was high and some of us figured we'd make a fortune so we leased a few plantations, but we didn't count on the boll weevil and our complete lack of knowledge of how cotton was grown. But it gave us a chance to get to know the people of Mississippi not as occupying soldiers but as equals. They're awfully fine people in Mississippi."

"How does cotton grow?"

"That's what we couldn't figure out," Dr. Forest said. "They're awfully fine people in Mississippi. They even speak the same language as we do. They're awfully fine people down there."

"Why do you keep on saying they're awfully fine people, Doctor Forest?"

"Because I'm trying to convince myself that some of them are human beings," Dr. Forest said. "And not only that, I'm still trying to figure out how the South won the war when they lost it. I swear to God I saw them lose it. I was there. I was there when they lost it and I was there when they were victorious. You boys are going to have to go down there and win it again."

"How we going to keep it won, Doctor Forest?"

"That's what I been trying to figure out since the war was over," Dr. Forest said, and then quietly with an edge to his voice, "since we lost it. The South, all of it, is filled with gentlemanly and gracious, loveable, kind, traditional people, very fine, very fine, and then along comes the Klu Klux Klan. The movies made heroes out of the Klan in a moving picture show called 'The Birth of a Nation.' They should have called it 'Lucifer Is Not Dead.'"

"Doctor Forest, you're going off the road."

Dr. Forest swung the Packard back on the road again. " 'How Lucifer is not dead,' " Dr. Forest said. " 'Or if he is I am in sorrowful, terrible error. I have been wronged. I am oppressed. I hate him that oppresses me. I shall either destroy him or he shall release me.' Do you boys know who wrote that?"

"Probably your friend Walt Whitman."

"That's right," Dr. Forest said. "To see so many Union dead," Dr. Forest said, studying the black fading wind of road. "To see so many Union dead and lose—"

"Who's to say who's right or who's wrong?" someone said.

Dr. Forest tightened his grip on the steering wheel so that his knuckles glowed white.

"Who said that?" Dr. Forest said.

"I did," Clancy Nublood said.

Dr. Forest turned his head away from the steering wheel, the Packard, the road, turned back to fix on Clancy, then his eyes turned much too slowly back to the road again as the Packard swept through Peapack, Liberty Corner down the Four Mile Hill, dipped into Basking Ridge, around Bernardsville, up the long grade toward Far Hills, but Dr. Forest never said anything, he just hung onto that wheel. Then at last, "Are you boys going all the way to Far Hills?"

"We might as well," Pete and Howie said.

When we got to Dr. Forest's house and piled out he said, "How are you boys going to get back to Prettyfields?"

"Hitchhike."

"Hitchhike," Dr. Forest said, reaching for his bag. "Then you better go by way of Bernardsville and see 'Frankenstein.' "

"Is that playing in Bernardsville?"

"Is it in talk and sound?" Charlie Peacock said.

"No, just in sound," Dr. Forest said. "But you'll like it. It will scare the ass off you," Dr. Forest said in army talk. Then he said, "Here's a quarter for each of you," and Dr. Forest metered out to us each in our dirty paws a bright twenty-five-cent piece, and Pete and Howie grabbed Dr. Forest's bag when he was not paying attention and dragged all those pills into the house for him and up the long, dark stairs and into the consulting room where the pills belonged.

"That's a daisy," Dr. Forest said as we all trooped like some lost platoon down the road toward the Liberty Theater in Bernardsville. "That's a perfect daisy."

We had to hike to Bernardsville because the road to Far Hills was a dead end, not a main highway, and after the stock market crash everyone in Far Hills except Dr. Forest had committed suicide so there was no traffic. "Doctor, canst thou not minister to a mind diseased, cleanse it of that stuff that lies so heavily on the brain?" Anyway the rich didn't call Dr. Forest before they committed suicide. That was Dr. Forest's way of making a good story out of the fact that several people did themselves in. Anyway there were no Rolls Royces today, no cars at all on that road. But it didn't take us long to walk into Bernardsville and the Liberty Theater where 'Frankenstein' was.

Outside there was a twenty-foot-high card cut-out of Frankenstein with shellac on his hair and the lower jaw festooned with blue electrodes. With his hands he was strangling a small blue-eyed blonde without many clothes on. There was a big sign that said, FRANKENSTEIN IN SOUND.

"What we'll do," Clancy said, "is that I'll buy one ticket with my own quarter, then I'll go in and let you guys in the exit. When you go in, you all hand me your quarter. That way it won't cost us nothing."

Clancy bought his ticket in the front and we went around to the exit and Clancy let us in. As we went past him he held out his hand for our quarters. We didn't give him our quarters. Charlie Peacock, Howie, and Pete spit in his hand.

"All right, all right, all right," Clancy said.

We all sat in the front row of the theater and Clancy was in back of us saying, "Look, you guys promised. You guys promised, didn't you?"

"I thought this picture was just in sound," Charlie Peacock said. "I didn't know there was any talk. It says outside just in sound."

"All right," Clancy said. "Give me your quarters."

We were at the part of the picture now where Boris Karloff is about to find Helen Twelvetrees hiding in the attic. "If you don't give me your quarters," Boris Karloff seemed to say. "If you don't give me your quarters—"

Meanwhile down in the cellar, Bela Lugosi was inventing a piece of Boris Karloff that had been missing. It was the piece of the brain that gives you human compassion and emotional maturity and without it you are a denizen of the jungle. Bela Lugosi looked at the missing part and wondered where Boris Karloff was now.

"How about my twenty-five centses?" Clancy said.

Now Bela Lugosi remembered that Boris Karloff had talked to him about his daughter, Helen Twelvetrees. The picture wasn't in talk but they talked with their eyes. Bela Lugosi certainly could talk with his eyes, he could make them stand on end, and Helen Twelvetrees talked with her breasts. She was very good with her breasts. Every time Boris Karloff said something that scared her she would heave her breasts.

It was a very modern picture. The makeup man had jewels of sweat stand out just above Helen Twelvetrees' breasts every time Boris Karloff got too close.

"How is the picture, Billy?"

"That was a good shot," I said.

"How about my twenty-five centses?" Clancy said.

"How do they do that?"

"They're working with two or more cameras," I said. "Now you're seeing Helen Twelvetrees through Boris Karloff's eyes."

"Has Bela Lugosi inserted the part yet that will give Boris Karloff emotional maturity?"

"No," I said.

I was the film critic and when we went to a picture I would

always comment on it as it went along. Everybody wanted to sit with me except for the time we went to see a Groucho Marx picture with a Hurricane Hutch short and I said, "Well, I don't know who I'll let sit with me next time," so nobody wanted to sit with me so I had to sit all by myself. Now I was a film critic again.

"Talk talk talk," Big Dick Gregory said. "I thought this picture was just in sound."

"You guys better give me your quarters," Clancy said.

Now Bela Lugosi, bigger, more sinister, more convincing than God, standing among the test tubes holding the emotional maturity piece of Boris Karloff that was missing, suddenly realized that Boris Karloff was in the bedroom with his daughter, Helen Twelvetrees. At the same time the director of the picture realized that they would get no place if Bela Lugosi didn't stop jumping up and down, so he had Bela Lugosi stare at the missing piece with feeling, more feeling! More feeling! And a subtitle came on the screen which said, "If only I had kept all the pieces in one pile."

Now the director cut upstairs to the bedroom where Boris Karloff was having sex every which way with Helen Twelvetrees and without his missing piece.

"How they doing, Cowboy?"

"Cinemawise, it's effective," I said. "Quite effective."

"I don't want all your twenty-five-cent pieces. Just enough to cover the risks. Cinemawise."

"Risks?"

"Yes. I could have been arrested for letting you in. Cinemawise.

"Risk pisk," Charlie Peacock said.

"Talk talk talk talk," Big Dick Gregory said.

Now a big shadow came from the back of the theater and touched us on the shoulders.

"You boys haven't paid," it said.

"We pay when we leave," Howie said.

"No, now."

"Talk talk talk," Howie said.

"No, now."

"We don't even know whether we want to buy it," Pete said. "Billy hasn't approved it."

"That's right," I said.

"We bought a Walt Disney picture last week," Pete said, "that was kitch."

"Slick slick slick," I said. "It's about time," Charlie Peacock said to the shadow in back of us, "that the audience took a stand."

"Outside on the cardboard cut-out, Helen Twelvetrees doesn't have a stitch on. In here after we've paid she's dressed to the nines. Cinemawise."

"You haven't paid," the big shadow said.

"If you people have something to settle, why don't you go outside? We're missing half the picture," Big Dick Gregory said.

"You haven't paid."

"They didn't pay me either," Clancy said.

"And anyway," Pete Nelson said to the ticket taker, "why is it with all these people in the theater you just pick on us?"

The usher turned the lights on and we were the only ones in the whole theater.

"That boy over there," the big shadow said, pointing to Clancy, "you're the only one that paid."

Clancy said, "Throw them all out."

When we picked ourselves up outside in the bright daylight we went into the lobby to get some popcorn by busting the popcorn machine, but the big man was still there so we went across the street and bought Seven For Sixes, Milky Ways, Mary Janes, chocolate eclairs, hearts, two of those, four of these, and a cupful of that. Then we all bought more vanilla and chocolate Milky Ways, three Hersheys, and a Necco. We ate everything up right away before Clancy got out, except the Milky Ways, they were frozen and we gnawed on those in front of the exit door waiting for Clancy. Then the big man came around again and asked us if we wanted to go in free.

"I was a boy myself once," he said.

"I don't believe it," Big Gregory said. "Do you have any proof? Anyway you made us miss the best part of the picture. Thanks anyway. You say you were a boy once yourself? All right, we'll go in."

"Anything to please a child," Pete and Eddie said.

Inside it was dark again and we were too late. Boris Karloff had already done to Helen Twelvetrees everything he had been going to do to her and when we got in they were both sitting on the edge of the bed looking relieved and philosophical just as Bela Lugosi came in with the missing part. As I said, the picture wasn't in talk, so Bela Lugosi couldn't come in and say, "Look here, I've invented the missing part." He just had to hold it up and they talked with their eyes. Pictures have lost a lot since people started talking with their mouths. Boris Karloff said with his eyes, "Ho ho ho, I see you've found the missing part, you inventor son of a bitch." And Helen Twelvetrees said with her eyes, "Ho ho ho, so we've been doing everything without the missing part. Is that possible, Father, you inventor prick?"

"How they doing, Cowboy?"

"Fine," I said. "Fine."

"The least you could do," Clancy said, "is give me a piece of the Milky Way."

"It's frozen. I can't break it."

"Don't eat it all up," Clancy said.

"I run all the way up here with the missing part, then I discover it's too late, you monster fornicator," Bela Lugosi said to Boris Karloff with his eyes.

"You're eating it all up," Clancy said.

"And you, Daughter," Bela Lugosi said with his eyes, "You couldn't even wait till I had finished inventing Frankenstein before you seduced him. You didn't even wait for the missing part." Helen Twelvetrees began to slink. She slinked around the edge of the bed and then she slunk forward with those big liquid wide-apart blue eyes that were the hallmark of Helen Twelvetrees. "Oh bug off, old man," she said to her father. "Frankenstein and me have got something going that's not only above nature, he being a mechanical man and all, it's not only a love that's above nature but it even seems to be, Father, above your inventions, above missing parts even." This was all said with Helen Twelvetrees' eyes and Bela Lugosi began to cry with his eyes.

"How's it, Billy?"

"Cinemawise, fine," I said. "Perfectly fine."

The picture ended on that note. Anyway I remember them

sitting on that bed crying. I don't know how they got Frankenstein to cry those real tears. I guess it was a copper tube they had
running up his back which came out someplace underneath his
eyebrows and there must have been a man under the bed
pumping out the water every time the director told him to. They
had good directors then. They don't make them like that
anymore.

Outside they asked me how the picture went and Clancy said,
"Has anyone got a piece of their frozen Milky Way left?" and I
said, "Cinemawise, fine, very fine."

But Clancy wondered.

"What do you wonder?" Howie Tordiff said.

We were hitchhiking now but nobody stopped.

"I wonder if the movie people get paid for making that junk"
Clancy said, and then another car went by.

"They could burn Hollywood down and we could make better
pictures at Prettyfields."

"Could we, Clancy?"

Another car came along, a blue Buick that I thought was going
to stop but it didn't.

"But where would we get the actors?" Big Gregory said.

"Hollywood did it without actors. Has anyone got more of
their frozen Milky Way left?" Clancy said. "Cowboy, have you got
any more of your frozen Milky Way left?"

"No," I said.

"No one seems to give a damn—no one gives a hang about
me," Clancy said.

A truck came up and stopped and we all climbed on the
tailboard and sat there on the tail gate all in a row and we

watched all of Bernardsville, Peapack, Basking Ridge, Liberty Corner, all of Somerset County retreating in a fleeting whirl of trees and brush and bridges, all mixed, confused, and swinging away like a kaleidoscope, a movie without talk or sound and shooting backwards.

Now we all answered Clancy. We all sang in talk and sound, shooting backwards, singing, passing over the Blue and into undulant and green rills of Somerset County as the sun quit, our song joined now by the steady sing of the tires. Together we sang, "No one here can love or understand me. Oh what hard luck stories they all hand me. Make my bed, light the light, I'll be home late tonight. Blackbird, bye bye." And then, "Mister Herbert Hoover says now's the time to buy. So let's have another cup of coffee and let's have another piece of pie."

"Clancy?"

"Yes?"

"We'll make it up to you." Again the soft sing of the tires made the silence bigger. "We'll not only give a damn about you, Clancy, we'll give a hang about you too."

In the moonshot dark someone said, "Nublood, bye bye."

When we jumped off the pick-up outside of Prettyfields, Eddie shouted to the fast-vanishing truck driver, "young man, that was a daisy."

As our pack skirted the forest, its Fall leaves yellow-reddening and moon-blued in the sharp October nightlight, Clancy trailed the pack. "The next time you guys pull a stunt like that, it will be your ass or mine."

"That's not a bad title for a song," Pete Nelson said.

When we got to the path of Prettyfields the pack scattered and vanished, then the sharp and vivid October moonspot lit up the distant far fields in myriad Fall somber-gay colors. Ah, yes, from my leaded window Prettyfields must have looked the way it looked, touched you the way it touched you long before the white man, before Frankenstein, even before picture shows talked with their eyes, before Everyman knew what drummer boys and little men were made of.

October light.

V

BENEATH A CIRCLING SPOTTED HAWK.

A bent plume of smoke curved in the empty blue, caused by the Old Packard driven by the older Dr. Forest. From where I lay with Beatrice you would have guessed the machine made no progress—that it—the plume of smoke—was an emission from some factory in the fields or the Hope Veterans Hospital, some stationary coal-fired plant idly polluting with innocent impunity—the phallic stack smoking a great endless cigar into a perfect and silent sky. And yet the source did move, and the movement was detectable as the elder Packard accomplished a hill, pulling its shadow, and puffed a heavy black sigh so that the tracing plume signed dark commas, question marks, and finally almost exclamation points as the plume thickened, as the Packard swerved crazily down Four Mile Hill, pushed by its shadow, near out of Bernardsville, near out of control, as Dr. Forest nudged the shift stick into neutral to allow the hulk to fly downward at panic speed—saves gas.

Saves time and clouds the illusion of time where we lay, with me thinking about the death of our teacher E. Mary Coca who died of loneliness, aloneness, who told us that everyone born into the world alive was either a little reader or a little writer. The only difference being that the writers were crazy. Why else would they submit to the lash of the critics when they could teach—sell opium or become a trader in jade? "But proceed with your oral history of Prettyfields, William. That's better than ending in prison or in the Harvard Business School. And proceed with your fantasy life, William. It's better to be crazy than lazy. It's best to write about what you imagine than about what at your age you do not know."

I knew, watching the Packard plume while lying with Beatrice beneath the marl oak. I knew what Beatee would be having her say.

"Your problem is, Billy, you're writer crazy," Beatee said. But my problem is I can't figure out how else you could do an oral history of Prettyfields. Your academy being in the shape it's in. A sane person would necessarily change the shape. But changing the shape doesn't change the truth."

"Our Master Auth, Philosophy I, says nothing is true."

"If nothing is true then that statement is true. If nothing is true then that's a truth. It sounds like Auth's mind is at sixes and sevens. Mine too."

"Not mine."

"But you're writer crazy."

"Is that good or bad?"

"Who knows? Considering the shape the country's in it's probably good."

"You sure?"

"Sure I'm sure."

"If you're sure then I'm happy."

"If you're happy I'm happy too."

"That's a song."

"No, it's a truth. Another truth your Auth missed," Beatee Keyes said. "A pack of Luckies for your thoughts, Billy."

"I was thinking that when the axemen entered this forest to kill, to fell these trees, that pine said bitterly to that oak, 'That axe handle was one of us.' "

"Can trees talk?"

"Of course."

"I read you, Billy."

Now a fresh, sharp gust of spanking wind hit the crest of the forest and the trees locked in song, swaying into neighbor space, embracing them standing straight, noble, indifferent as the wind abated in a faint sibilant hiss.

"Oh boy."

"You call that tree-talking, Billy?"

"Of course."

"I read you, Billy."

Beatrice fumbled into the stuff of her handbag and withdrew a flat tine of Egyptian Ovals with a myriad assortment of purple, gold, magenta and cork tips. She tapped a cork tip on the forest floor and watched out over the somnolent Blue, the still and unmoving Blue, as though the stream, having paused here at the marl oak, might reverse and go back home; tapping the cigarette on the forest floor, thinking, Jesus, what are boys made of that they hold converse with trees and the river while I sit? Maybe the male is of a strange and different species. At least this could be true of Prettyfields boys' academy. "Could it?"

"Could it what?"

"I read you, Billy, but could it be true that the boys of Prettyfields are different?"

"Different than what?"

"Than boys who are not separated from the girls of home, from family—different than boys who are not sentenced to a private boarding school. Is Prettyfields a quaint name for a prison?"

"Of course."

"Is there no difference?"

"None that I can think of—off-hand."

"What about—" Beatrice finally lit her Egyptian Oval and blew out a cloud of off-color smoke—"I read you, Billy, but what about—?"

"You lit the wrong end."

Beatrice tried another, this time a gold tip, and got the right end in her mouth. "What about the lack of bars?"

"You mean no booze?"

"No, I mean no steel bars on the windows."

"Prettyfields makes up for it by putting bars on the soul."

"Billy, you never stick to the point. You always wander off into some highfalutin pronouncement. Remember, these are hard times, Billy." Beatee watched around the forest as though searching for some answer to the hard times, the Great Depression, her eyes alight like some ancient Greek nubile mistress questing the solution in the Fates in the rank on rank of protective rear guard soldier trees that encircled the marl oak—the last redoubt and bastion against the axe called civilization (the handle was one of us!). "Not only hard times, Billy, but the indifference of people who've got it all." She paused as though in abrupt wonder at the arboreal world above, twisting and untwisting her gold-flecked braids. "Those that don't give a damn about the likes of us."

I wanted to tell Beatee, the blonde and blue-eyed concerned angel daughter of the general storekeeper Charlie Keyes, the beautiful child Beatrice who lay gently under the lightshadow gibe of the marl oak, I wanted to tell her, and I did, "Beatee, I care about the likes of you, and it will all be in the book, along with the likes of us." And then I said, "But when are we going to do it?"

"We already did it."

"When are we going to do it again?"

"When you get rested," Beatee said.

"I'm rested."

"I'm not that kind of a girl."

"You were a while ago."

"Women change."

"Me too."

"You mean, Billy, you don't want to do it now?"

"Men change."

"Did I say something wrong?"

"No."

"Oh, come on, Billy, you've got to play according to the rules and regulations. A lady is not supposed to want to do it."

"Is that right?"

"Of course it's right. A rule is a rule."

"I don't want to play."

"I'm sick of the game too, Billy. I'll do it if you're game."

"I'm game."

"I'm game if you're game."

"No more talking. Let's get to the business at hand."

"I read you, Billy. Let's see what's up."

And we did, there in the last redoubt beneath the gathering of the last stand of tree, did it in the last island of the last vine, last root, last Johnny-come-lately and Judy pop-up flowering. We sweated the great sweet act—the lurch, the parry, the thrust, the acrobatics of love in the mink-brown woods along the wide Blue on the soft black floor of the forest beneath the unmoving broil of sun, beneath the high wind hiss music and dry leaf clash of the wild forest band so that you maybe felt that time must have a stop, that this adagio and ballet and swift accompaniment would quit and leave you sprawled naked and alone—like that. But the descent was smooth and loving, soundless and gentle so that the ending stroke of soft hands was right. And all was right as loving can be.

"All right?"

"All right."

Now there was the picking up of the pieces—the gathering of all the loose ends. In the struggle of love it must amaze the encircling angels and cherubim to see the disarray, the damage, the clutter and the chaos to the law and order, the broken comb, the busted mirror reflecting back a bleared, spent image, the scattered blood of lipstick, the waft of leaked perfume hinting at poison gas warfare, the immobile bodies in the awkward angles of the dead. The litter of the battlefield. This is where the brave died. This is where the stout-hearted stood.

"You sure you're all right?"

"Yes, I'm sure I'm all right."

Going back to Charlie Keyes' I said, "Did you know, Beatee, an Indian believes that he is one with nature, that a disjoining with nature is the only tragedy. Of course a tree cannot listen, talk, look, as we talk, look, listen, but we cannot bloom like a tree, spread like a tree, sing with the wind like a tree, dance in the wind like a tree—in a quick breeze a forest is a thousand dancers dancing. We cannot move like a tree nor get to know and feel any certain place like a tree surrounded by its child seedlings who never leave home. A tree is a piece that fits a place. A man is a missing jigsaw piece wandering under a tree searching for a place to fit."

"Jesus, Billy."

"Why 'Jesus, Billy'?"

"If I read you, they're going to lock you up."

"I'm only telling you what the world believed before the white man came. Ask any Indian."

"I don't know any, Bill."

"Don't get mad."

"Who's mad?"

On our way to Charlie Keyes' we paused at an oxbow of the Blue to raid a bramble of elderberries until we were streaming purple from the juice, robed in pope-purple from the juice. "Who's mad?"

"If I read you, you're going through a phase, Billy, when you're mad at everyone, everything. You'll feel better in the morning."

"It is not madness, madam, that I speak. There are more things in heaven and earth than are dreamt of in your philosophy. William Shakespeare said that."

"He did, did he? Jesus, Billy, I'm not interested in William Shakespeare. As much as I try, I'm interested in Billy Catchfield. I'm interested in us." The grape of elderberry bled like fresh blood down Beatee's face as she gorged on the enemy. She would leave no feast for the foxes. "I could be dead for all you know. I could be dead for all you care," Beatee said.

When we got back on the asphalt, our frost-bearded Dr. Forest gave us a lift in his Packard to the tune of his Civil War adventures. He was that old, he was that wise.

"Where to?"

"Charlie Keyes'."

"You look like you've axe-murdered the Prettyfields faculty. Has the revolution begun in Earnest?"

"Where? Oh, you mean in earnest."

"That's what I said. Or is your blood elderberry juice?"

"Elderberry juice."

"Elderberry juice?" Dr. Forest's Packard proceeded with the funereal stateliness, almost rectitude, of a great ship on a calm, vast sea. Now he leaned his sage head forward, close against the windshield to see the future road, but came up with time past. "Elderberry juice? We New Jersey Volunteers all got drunk on self-made elderberry wine just before the Confederates burst through and unhinged our right flank at Shiloh. It was touch and go before we closed the gap. The Reb was pouring through like a dam had burst. I attribute our so-called victory at Shiloh solely to the virtues of elderberry wine. But my children, the dead do not go easy. The gap was shut in the Union line with the bodies of the young Union dead like piled sandbags against that gray flood. My dear comrades' bodies that filled the gap that saved our army, that saved a cause. Cause? What cause? The Black is still held by the invisible chain to the indifferent wall and the sheeted dead still defame the cross by burning it in Biloxi." There was a long silence, then, "How would you like to go and see Elizabeth Mary Coca?"

"She's dead. Can I shift for you?"

"Yes, go ahead. I'll double-clutch, Cowboy, and then you shift down. I know Elizabeth is dead. I thought I'd stop at the Millington Funeral Home and honor Elizabeth's remains. Are you people game?"

"I'm game."

"Me too."

"First you'll have to wash off all that blood. If the Prettyfields faculty turns up dead—shift, Billy—you two would be prime suspects and I'd be an accessory after the fact. What were you two doing in the woods before your elderberry feast? I withdraw the question. Do you realize that most among the Union dead never had sex? At least that was true in the New Jersey Volunteers. They draft for the legal murder called war much too young. They draft those who have not lived. We should only draft—do you feel some rain?"

"Not enough to put the top up."

"We should only draft those who have lived. Those who have something to be dead for. Those who are not too young but those who are too old to die—fifty and up. That would—do you want the top up yet?"

"Not yet."

"Drafting the old would cancel all wars. Then the Confederates would have thought ten times before attacking the flat at Sumter and starting a war. The impossible looks easy if you can order the young to try it."

"Think so?"

"Know so. We can put the top up when we pull into Happy Hooligan's."

"Do you need gas?"

"No, but you need to wash up." George Hooligan came trotting through the rain as I pulled up the emergency brake.

"Fill 'er up, Happy," Dr. Forest said. "These people want to wash up. They've just murdered half the faculty at Prettyfields—"

"I'm sorry to hear that."

"—and we want to remove the evidence. Let them have the key to the restroom. Restroom?" Dr. Forest mused as the rain drained from the end of his nose in a waterfall on to his Walt Whitman beard. "Restroom? Have they? Have they got beds in there?"

Beatrice went to hers and I went to his and when we got out, Happy Hooligan had the Packard top up and was stroking gas up into the high-gravity-feed glass tank. The glass tank held ten gallons, so the Packard had already taken ten. With a glass tank you could see you were getting full measure. Each gallon was marked on the glass tank on a descending scale. The catch was, Dr. Forest insisted, that they only had to pump up nine gallons in the morning to get ten gallons by the high noon heat. Gasoline expands. Money contracts. Happy Hooligan delights. The high-octane gas was red, the low-octane gas blue, so that a Standard Oil of New Jersey service station looked like a garish roadside carnival. "The glass tank is disappearing," Dr. Forest said, "but big oil will discover other ways to turn the knife."

"Think so?"

"Know so. Do you think we should put up the side curtains?"

In the pelting rain we got out and put up the remains of the side curtains. The isinglass curtains were torn to ribbons. The buttonholes didn't fit, so all our tattered sails were at half mast when we docked the Packard clipper at the funeral home, all flags flying, but looking like we had lost an engagement with an ironclad off Sand Hook or abandoned the scattered fleet at Trafalgar—forgive us, Lord Nelson, we were sore afraid.

Inside the funeral home smelled high of carbolic acid and the benign sweet smell of the innocent dead. Dr. Forest grouped us around the plastic-flowered coffin, and as though we were linked hand in hand at some princess of the realm's wake we all watched down in quiet stupor at the new-enameled face of what once might have been our Elizabeth Mary Coca.

Dr. Forest raised his free hand in a gesture at once of benediction, blandishment—perplexed—"Do you understand, my children, do you understand the blackness, the infinity, the empty void of death?"

"No."

Dr. Forest led us from the cold of the sepulcher out into the now no rain. We tumbled over the running board, climbed over the toolbox and both sat amidships. Dr. Forest climbed aboard, shut his door and stared, searching ahead over the steering wheel. "Neither do I," he said.

At Charlie Keyes' store the big rain had given way to a quiet sun. Dr. Forest touched us good-bye, placed the Packard gear shift in low, but before he quit Charlie Keyes', before he jerked away in a barn-burning exhaust pillar of smoke, he told the Packard and quietly too confided to the universe, "Neither do I, my children, and no man I know has reckoned it yet."

Now Dr. Forest wonderously disappeared, magically vanished in the Packard smoke trick; magically vanished in old Dr. Forest's ancient Packard miracle of barn-burning smoke.

Moving away, our Dr. Forest, beneath his mottled-with-age hawked nose, over his Whitmanesque beard, softly announced to the unseen, the unseeing cold blue lake above, floating scudding white clouds, "A spotted hawk swoops by and accuses me. He complains of my gab—but I too am untamed. I send my barbaric yawp over the roofs of the world. I shake my white locks. I depart as air—but failing to find me, keep encouraged. Missing me one place, search another. I stop somewhere, waiting for you. *Allons!* The road is before us. I give you my love, more precious than money. Will you give me of yourself? Will you travel with me? Shall we stick by each other as long as we live?"

Now as we passed the sun-shot bottled cider on Charlie Keyes' porch, "We read you, Doctor Forest," Beatee Keyes said.

GERALD HASLAM

The Man Who Cultivated Fire
& Other Stories

VOLUME XI

CAPRA PRESS
1987

Cover design by Francine Rudesill.
Designed and typeset in Garamond by Jim Cook
SANTA BARBARA, CALIFORNIA

LIBRARY OF CONGRESS CATALOGING-IN-PUBLICATION DATA
Eastlake, William.
Prettyfields: a work in progress.
(Capra back-to-back; v. 11)
No collective t.p. Titles transcribed from individual title pages.
Texts bound together back to back and inverted.
I. Haslam, Gerald W. Man who cultivated fire, and other stories. 1987.
II. Title.   III. Title: Man who cultivated fire, and other stories.
PS3555.A7P7 1987   813'.54   87-11791
ISBN 0-88496-266-0 (pbk)

PUBLISHED BY
CAPRA PRESS
Post Office Box 2068
Santa Barbara, California 93120

CONTENTS

THE MAN WHO CULTIVATED FIRE

The Man Who Cultivated Fire

THAT MAD ARMENIAN IS CULTIVATING FIRE,"
my grandmother warned Mrs. Alcala that morning. "He
is a menace. *Muy* peligroso," she nodded. "He is a *very*
dangerous man."

Mrs. Alcala, even older than Grandma and not given to strong
talk, remained unconvinced. "Ah, Lupe," she smiled, "you carry on
about nothing. Leave the old man alone. He harms no one."

"He harms *me*," Grandma insisted. "He is loco. He walks
around that terrible, overgrown yard of his talking to himself. And
singing sometimes. Do you understand, *singing!* A grown man."

"No, no," Mrs. Alcala disagreed pleasantly, leaning on the
unpainted fence that separated her small yard from ours, "the man
is a poet. He simply recites his poems as he works in his yard. He
is a good man, I tell you, a kind one. Doesn't he give us all fruit?"

"I would never eat it," snapped my grandmother. "Poisoned, you
know."

9

Mrs. Alcala couldn't suppress a chuckle. "Nonsense, I have eaten it for years."

Grandma only snorted. She had often commented to me on her neighbor's poor health. "Alright, Esperanza," she finally responded, "alright, but that madman is also growing fire in his yard and when our neighborhood has been consumed and we are all burned to *chicharrones,* out on the street with no houses, then you will agree with me. Everyone will. But it will be too late!" Grandma's voice was rising and her head was bobbing as she spoke. "One day those weeds of his will burst into flames! Mark my words!"

"Ah, Lupe," smiled our neighbor, "you must control yourself. Calm down. Mr. Samuelian grows weeds, not fire. He waters them and they grow huge and green. They harm no one. Calm yourself, my friend, or you'll burst a vein."

Grandma seemed nearly as angry at Mrs. Alcala's tranquil response as she was at the Armenian. Her nostrils were flared when she puffed, "A singing madman is cultivating weeds into a fire hazard, and Esperanza Alcala speaks to me as though I am a child. He would have *long* ago been committed to the madhouse if this was the *American* section of town, but here...," she was sputtering in her anger.

"It's *that* again, is it," Mrs. Alcala remarked sharply, her smile gone. "I have work to do." She turned and walked as quickly as her two canes allowed into her small bungalow.

I understood her sudden impatience. Although everyone in our family agreed that my grandmother was a saint—she attended Mass daily and never failed to receive Holy Communion—she was not altogether popular among those who lived nearest her. In fact,

Mrs. Alcala was the neighbor who most tolerated Grandma, although Mr. Samuelian, whose house bordered ours on the other side, also tried to be friendly but she would have nothing to do with him.

Grandma's designs about him had begun long before I moved in with her, or so I'd heard from Flaco, Mrs. Alcala's grandson who lived down the street. He told me he'd heard that shortly after the poet had moved next door, he and my grandmother had been talking across the fence when the subject of nationality had arisen. Mr. Samuelian had said that although his parents were immigrants, he was an American, born up the highway in Fresno. Grandma had responded that she was Spanish. "Oh," he'd asked, "what part of Spain are you from?"

My grandmother was born on a ranch near Fort Tejon and had lived most of her life right here in Bakersfield. "My *people* were from Spain," she'd replied sharply, and not too candidly, since my uncle'd told me that our family had lived in the state of Sonora for several generations before coming north to California. To a woman like Grandma, though, one who claimed to be pure Castilian, Mr. Samuelian's response had been challenge enough: "Oh," and he had smiled.

Watching Mrs. Alcala disappear into her house that morning, my grandmother turned to me and remarked, "Too bad. Esperanza was such a good woman but now her mind is slipping. *Que lá*stima." She shook her head sadly. "She cannot see the danger." After a moment, Grandma sighed, "Oh well, help me with these onions, hijo." I toted a double armload from the garden into our cabin.

And it really was *our* cabin, mine and Grandma's. After my

mother and father had divorced, I'd moved in with her while Momma traveled to Los Angeles to find work. By the time she'd located a job, I was enrolled in Our Lady of Guadalupe School and it was decided that I should complete the academic year before moving. Came summer, and Momma had determined that East L.A. was not a place to raise a boy, so I became Grandma's permanent companion.

Almost the first friend that I'd made after moving in was Mr. Samuelian. Most kids in the neighborhood haunted his yard, and he seemed to delight in our company, offering fruit from his trees and free run of his property, along with a smattering of advice, always lightly offered and easy to accept. Like Flaco's cussing: "You hold in mouth what I scrape off my shoe." Flaco watched his language after that.

Then there was the time Mike Padilla, who attended public school, said he was going to beat up a Jew in his class because he was a Christ killer. Without heat, Mr. Samuelian asked, "How old is he?"

"Like me," Mike replied, "twelve."

"Well, Christ has been dead nearly two thousand years, so I think the boy is falsely accused. Besides, my Bible tells me that the sins of mankind killed Jesus, so if you sin by assaulting a classmate, you become a Christ killer, don't you?"

"I do?" Mike blinked. Mr. Samuelian handed him an orange.

Because I lived next door, I saw more of the poet than the other kids. He owned a tiny shack on a long, narrow lot covered with fruit trees and towering weeds, both of which he carefully nurtured. As much as we all loved his fruit, it was his weeds that most attracted us, the very weeds my grandmother so hated. They

were our jungle—lush and varied, tall, flowered, feathered; short, wrinkled, sprawling. High as my head, weeds verdant, weeds luxuriant; soft beneath our feet, carpet, wall and roof of weeds, with only tunnels to the fruit trees cut through them. Everything in the yard, weeds and trees, grown rich from daily water and frequent fertilizer.

In fact, Mr. Samuelian himself at first seemed secondary to his marvelous yard to most of us kids. He was a small man with an explosion of silver hair, with eyebrows as thick and unruly as his weeds and a sweeping, yellowed mustache from which short cigars often wiggled when he talked. He cultivated his yard each morning and evening, spouting lines from poems as he toiled, then stopping to jot them with the stub of a pencil into the pocket notebook he carried.

During midday's heat he would disappear into his shack, and we never disturbed him then. From my yard, I could hear the clatter of typewriter keys over the whir from the large evaporative cooler on his roof. Once a week or so he'd amble to the bus stop down the street balancing an armload of books to return to the public library, then he'd be back with another of them later. "What's *in* those books?" Grandma would demand, not of Mr. Samuelian, of course, but of me. "It's not normal for a man to read so much," she'd assert before I could frame an answer, closing the discussion.

Us kids knew what was in them, or at least some of them, because Mr. Samuelian told us about them—something Grandma suspected but could not prove. "He *talks* to you," she would accuse.

"Sure," I'd reply, "about baseball. He thinks the Cubs will win this year."

"Hah!" she would snort. "You'd better stay away from him. He is loco and he will twist you." Grandma was too wise to absolutely forbid that I speak with our neighbor, but she kept an eye on me.

We did occasionally discuss baseball, but only occasionally. The poet talked to us about lots of things—why our sky is no longer blue, how a whale can breathe, what the Constitution guarantees, where the water we drink comes from—lots of things. When workers in the grape fields up in Delano went on strike, my family—Momma, who was visiting, and Grandma—agreed that the strikers and the priests supporting them were communists. I didn't know for certain what communists were but I could discern from the discussion's tone that they were very bad indeed. My questions were dismissed, so I wandered next door to ask Mr. Samuelian if the strikers were communists and what it meant if they were.

His bushy eyebrows quivered like angry caterpillars and he handed me a pomegranate from his tree. "Look at it, my boy," he exclaimed, "a little leather pouch filled with rubies!" I giggled. "Now, who told you the people in the fields are communists?"

"Momma and Grandma."

"Ah, and you don't know what 'communist' means?"

He cleared his throat and plopped down onto the wooden garden chair under a tree near his front door. "Well," he said, "it is one of those words with no precise meaning."

"I don't get it." I was pulling leathery peel from the red fruit he'd given me.

Mr. Samuelian smiled. "I mean, my boy, that people know the word has the power to hurt others, so they apply it to anyone or anything they don't like. Some people, of course, follow the

teachings of a man named Karl Marx. They are not only called communists by others but they also call themselves that.

"But the men and women striking the grape growers don't read Karl Marx. Very likely, they don't have time to read anything at all. They are simply tired of being poor and misused, so they demand higher wages and human dignity. Higher wages for them, however, means less profits for growers, so they in turn call the strikers communists to discredit them. Do you understand?"

I wasn't certain. "It's like calling someone a bad name?" I asked, after crunching a mouthful of the juicy red beads.

"Exactly." He thrust a finger into the sky. "Some of the growers—the small ones—like the strikers themselves, struggle for better lives. Others...," he shrugged his shoulders and raised his eyebrows. "...well, they are rich and wish to become richer. The rich farmers pretend they are also poor, and the strikers seem unable to tell the difference, so each side calls the other names."

I stood before him and chewed on what he said. Then I asked, "What about 'sticks and stones can break my bones, but words will never hurt me'?" I bit into the pomegranate once more and a crimson stream shot from the fruit, causing me to giggle.

Mr. Samuelian ducked quickly. "You are dangerous," he chuckled. Then he ran his fingers through his wild silver hair. "Ah, to be young," he smiled.

"To answer your question, I'm afraid that words can hurt you far more than sticks and stones normally do. What if I go to your school and tell the nuns that you are a thief? That label would stay with you as long as you remained at Guadalupe. The teachers would not trust you, and soon even your friends might begin to doubt you, because that word not only means you have stolen, it

predicts that you will steal again. You would suffer from the effects of the label, 'thief,' long after a broken bone had healed," he nodded several times. "Long after."

After a moment, he continued: "The same thing is true of 'communist.' It is a word that might haunt you to your grave. Employers might not hire you. Friends might avoid you. Even the government might hound you—all because of that word."

"No lie?"

"No lie, indeed," he answered.

Impulsively, I asked, "What if someone said someone else was crazy?"

A slight grin curved under Mr. Samuelian's mustache. "Well, it depends on who says it. If said by a fool, it is dismissed. On the other hand, if a doctor says a person is crazy, that word can be a heavy burden." He spoke earnestly, then his tone brightened. "Fortunately, fools, not doctors, usually say such things. Listen carefully to those you hear using it, then check how many are doctors."

"Oh," I said. I caught on right away to what that made my grandmother, so I pursued the subject no farther. Instead, I finished eating my pomegranate.

When I returned home that day, I heard my grandmother lecturing into the telephone: "...but I tell you the man has let his yard go to weeds. The entire *neighborhood* could burn. He is a terrible menace." She eyed the tell-tale pomegranate stains around my mouth as she spoke those words.

Once she hung up, Grandma thrust her chin in my direction. "Now that wild man will *have* to conform—or get out," she asserted. "I have called the Fire Marshal and he is sending an

Inspector." In triumph, she strode from the house to inform Mrs. Alcala.

The next day the Inspector arrived, and I joined my grandmother with most of the other neighbors gathered next to the official white car in front of Mr. Samuelian's yard. Shortly, the two men—one stern in a blue uniform and white cap, the other pleasant in rumpled khakis—were wandering together through the dense foliage. When they neared the front of the yard, I heard the blue-clad man order brusquely, "These'll all have to come down. We don't allow weeds in Bakersfield."

"But they aren't weeds," responded our neighbor pleasantly.

"What do you mean, these aren't weeds? I can see what they are: weeds!" snapped the Inspector.

"What is a weed, then?" was Mr. Samuelian's gentle reply.

The uniformed man stopped walking, positioned his hands on his hips, and growled, "You trying to get smart with me?"

"It is a serious question," the old poet assured him. "What is a weed?"

The officer glanced away from our neighbor toward all of us gawking there by the fence, then returned his gaze to Mr. Samuelian. "It's something that grows no matter what and where you don't want it or need it, I guess, and *these* are weeds."

"But I planted most of them. They all grow where I want them, and I'm pleased with them. How can they be weeds?"

"Because," the blue-clad man explained with tight lips, "a weed is a weed, and those things are all weeds, everything but that rose on the fence there, anyway."

"That is a wild rose. It grows where I don't want it no matter what."

The face above the uniform reddened and seemed to swell then. For a moment I thought the Inspector would grab Mr. Samuelian, but instead he jerked a pad from one pocket and began scrawling into it. "You have exactly seven days to cut these damn weeds," he spat, "or we'll do it for you at *your* expense. See that it's done!"

Our neighbor simply nodded.

The officer thrust his pad toward Mr. Samuelian, who dutifully signed it, then accepted his copy. Spinning away and not saying a word, the Inspector—eyebrows knit in a tight V, the tips of his ears maroon—stalked to his car. He seemed to leap inside, started the engine, then roared away.

The old poet did not move. He watched the vehicle trail dust as it disappeared, then glanced at all of us gathered on the dirt between his yard and the street. Finally, he shrugged, put his copy of the ticket in a pocket, and smiled at us. "Would anyone like a pomegranate?" he asked.

Everyone began talking and laughing at once, flooding onto his yard, everyone but my grandmother. I wouldn't have noticed her wandering along toward our house except that Mr. Samuelian's eyes followed her. "The poor woman," he said.

The World Sucks

IT'S ONE OF THEM DAYS, MAN, WHEN WE
been smokin' dope, drinkin' wine, and drivin' cars backwards
in the parkin' lot. No jobs, of course, or at least nothin' worth
a rusty fuck. Ain't gonna wash no lousy dishes for no minimum
wage. No pearl divin' for me, man. Hell, I can buy a bag of weed,
smoke half myself, cut it with good old Liptons, and sell it to some
polyester cowboy for twice what I paid. Free enterprise, man.

Not this day, though. We run out of dope quick and drain the
last of the wine. Me and Cleve and Artie and T.J. we finally give
up and drive over to Kentucky Fried Chicken to beg some bread.
We park the old Chevy—it so battered that it looks like an armored
personnel carrier—across the street and leave T.J. in it, then set
up shop on the sidewalk, man. For a long time nobody shows,
which is strange at K.F.C. where the yahoos usually congregate to
grease and fart.

Just when I'm ready to go lookin' for aluminum cans or old ladies to roll, this ancient coot hobbles up the street. I poke Artie and hiss, "Pension check, man." He nods. We wait until grandpa eats his chicken, then nail him when he trucks out the door.

" 'Scuse me, man," I say, holdin' my coat collar and droopin' my eyes. He keeps on truckin'.

I reach out and tug at one of his sleeves. " 'Scuse me, man," I repeat.

He stops. "Eh?"

I turn on my chin tremble and give him one a my patented T.B. coughs. "Could you spare some change, man?" I whimper. "My wife's like nine months pregnant, man, and she's over in that car there"—I point feebly toward the Chevy—"and we're stranded here in Sacramento. My job didn't come through, man, and we need to get back to L.A. Can you help us? Please." Off to the side, Artie and Cleve they're fightin' not to laugh. *Figh-tin'*. Too fuckin' much.

The old man follows the line of my droopin' finger, man, till his eyes catch the car. T.J., that I'd pulled this scam with before, he's sittin' in it with a bandana around his head. He gives us a limp little faggot wave.

That pensioner squints. "What the hell *is* that?" he demands in this high pitched voice.

"What?" I asks, not likin' his tone.

"That clown in the car?"

"That's my wife, man!"

The old guy rolls his eyes. "Tell 'er to shave," he advises, then trots away.

"Hey!" I holler. "How 'bout my quarter?" He don't pay no attention to me, man.

"Shit!" I say to Artie and Cleve. "We shoulda robbed him, man."

"Ohhh nooo," chants Artie, "no more of the robbin' action. Uhn-uhn. Not for the kid. Last time was too close. People do not know how to act when you rob 'em, act crazy, make you hurt 'em, then bang! you are in the slammer. Ohhh nooo. Not for the kid."

"Sheee," Artie," Cleve points out, "we need some jingle, bro'. Got to buy some taste."

Artie keeps shakin' his head. "The kid does not need no county-issue overalls. Orange is not my color."

That's how bad things can get, man. All our unemployment checks stopped. The eagle not due to shit till the first, man, and none of us workin'. Got to scuffle to stay alive. No decent jobs in this burg, man.

"Pssst!" I hear T.J. hiss from across the street. I look at him and he points up the street. Hot shit! A bundle of polyester waddlin' toward K.F.C., man. He steps like he's crossin' a pasture, like he's tryin' to avoid cow plops, fancy prancin' man. I'm thinkin' paper, not change, when I spot this hayseed.

We wait outside like buzzards circlin' while the chubby dude orders. He's beautiful, man. White shoes, white belt, both shiny plastic. Maroon slacks, maroon-and-white checkered coat, white shirt, white tie: all of it stone polyester. He hit all the fuckin' blue-light specials at K-Fuckin'-Mart. On a hot day, his clothes would melt, leavin' a big puddle of plastic, man, with a naked fat dude in the middle. "Look at that cherry tie, man," I say, whistlin' through my teeth.

"My man clean," coos Cleve, then he laughs: "Chi chi chi!"

"Looks like he hit a price war between Goodwill and St. Vincent de Paul," chuckles Artie. Me and Cleve crack up, man.

"Ooops," I says, "here he comes."

Polyester waddles outa K.F.C., a paper bag in one hand, a cup of cola in the other—high dinin' in the big city, man. I assemble my tragic-husband face and clutch my collar with one hand. " 'Scuse me, man," I mumble. He stops. So far, so good. "I got a bad problem. See, my wife's pregnant, man, and we're stranded here without no work livin' in that car over there."

Right on cue, T.J., coverin' his five-o'clock-shadow with the bandana, waves. "She's pregnant, man," I go on, "and I gotta get gas money to take her home. Can you loan me a few bucks, man?"

"Huh?" says Poly, lookin' baffled. We can sure pick 'em, man. I go through the whole damn routine again.

"Naw," he says when I finish, givin' me a hayseed grin. He's thinkin' about that fried chicken sure as hell. Got to get to his grease.

"No?"

"Nope." Off he starts waddlin'.

I follow him and debate whether to knock the fucker out and steal his chicken, man, or give the scam one more try. "Hey wait, man," I call.

He stops.

"Wanna buy some dope?" I ask, all of a sudden inspired.

"Dope?"

"Yeah, wacky-backy, weed, grass, shit, mary-jew-wanna." Ah-ha! I was right.

"How much?" Think quick, man. How much can Poly afford? "Ten bucks a joint."

"Real marijuana?" His little eyes squint.

"Rio Grande Red, man, the best," I confide.

"Gimme two."

I shoulda charged twenty, man, damnit. This dude is green. "Artie," I call, "my man needs a couple jays."

"Sure thing," Artie answers, fishin' two Lipton's specials from his breast pocket, "the kid comes through." We'd finished the real shit two hours before, man.

Chunky buns pays off and slips the two elongated tea bags quickly into a breast pocket, lookin' both ways. Behind me I hear Cleve:"Chi-chi-chi!" The maroon drawers and checkered jacket fade up the street, man. Cleve observes softly, "Clean like a mothahfuckah, bro'. Chi chi chi!"

"Hey, Cleveland," Artie observes, "*we* are not exactly wearin' the good ropes, man. The kid does not dig these damn ol' fatigues."

"At least yours don't expose no tattoos," I point out. "Mine're air-conditioned, man."

"Chi-chi-chi!"

"What're you so damn happy about, man?" I ask Cleve.

"M-O-N-Y, money. We in the chips, bro'," he replies.

T.J. wanders over. "How much?" he asks.

"Twenty skins, man," I tell him.

"Good. I'm hungry. Let's go grease some chili."

"Got to buy us some taste," Cleve urges.

"Naw, got to have some chili action for the kid."

I agree. "Yeah, man, let's eat somethin', then we can pick up a long dog with the change, kinda mellow out. Let's hit Nell's Chili

Palace, man." We all pile in my short, man, and off we go. Zoom to doom, man, chili here we come.

Nell looks like she not only *can* go two-out-of-three with the Masked Marvel, man, but like she just *has*. "What do you jokers want?" she demands. Her ankles are thick and she walks on the outside of her shoes, feet slopin' away from each other like they got noses. Her shoulders are fat. Artie, the ladies' man, says she's got a spider tattooed on one tit, but I'm sure as hell never checkin'.

"We came in just for your company, man," I answer.

She gives me the eye. "Buzz off," she says. "You characters got money this time?"

"We got the green," big Cleve replies.

"Let's see." Her eyes're slit into these fleshy folds, little dots in the middle, man.

I flash the ten spot.

"Okay, one chili each comin' up."

While she scuttles into the kitchen, man, T.J. whispers out the side of his mouth, "How'd you like to be stranded on a desert island with Nell, man?"

"Chi-chi-chi! Who you bullshittin', bro'? Ain' no broad *you* won' hit on. Besides, ask my man Artie. She look better'n that broad he with las' night."

"Anything looks better'n that beauty, man," I add. Artie has screwed every waitress on skid row, accordin' to him anyways. He was the same way in Nam, always at the dispensery because he had the fuckin' clap, but it didn't slow him down much. It's a wonder he hasn't caught fuckin' leprosy, man.

"Hey! Hey! Do not cap on the kid," says the great lover.

"Besides, even if Sally did not look too good last night, she can suck-start a semi."

"And she *do*," adds Cleve crackin' us up, man. "Chi-chi-chi!"

Nell delivers the chili—givin' Artie a big grin, ignorin' the rest of us—and we grease. Good shit, man, Nell's chili makes it worth all the bad-mouth she hands out. I'd hate to have to kiss her to get it, though. That'd be your basic moral crisis.

On a bench in the park, fulla chili and feelin' fine, man, but I don't know, it kinda gets me. I mean, can you believe, man, that all these clowns struttin' by, can you believe that all these assholes, got jobs? I mean, look at 'em: faggots and fartknockers and foreigners, man, and they got real jobs, rollin' in the green, not no minimum wage. They ain't sellin' aluminum cans. Dudes buzzin' by in fancy cars with fine lookin' bitches, man, all of 'em workin', livin' high. I don't know what the fuck's goin' down, man. I don't get it.

"Let's go hit on some bitches," I suggest, wantin' to clear my mind, man, get that shit outta there. "Gotta party hearty, man."

"Yeah, man," grins Artie, "let's go hit on Sally."

"I said bitches, man, not dogs."

"Chi-chi-chi!"

"Do not cap on the kid," advises Artie.

"Maybe we can find a place to live, you guys," says T.J. "I'm sick of humpin' it under the fuckin' freeway. Too fuckin' windy. It sucks."

"Le's go kick somebody's ass," suggests Cleve real pleasantly.

"Big Cleve got to get him some county-issue threads, man," croons Artie. "Not for the Kid. No orange coveralls, thank you." He bows like he just met the fuckin' queen, man.

"Sheee'."

So we drift, man, no place in particular to go, but it's early and I don't want to go back to our humble abode, man, under the freeway. Not so much a pad, man, as a path. We got two old couches under there, a table and a couple chairs, even a tent. The cops know we're there, but so far they left us alone. It's a noisy fucker, though, man, and windy. Funny thing is, it's probably better than that flophouse where I was crashin' before I got laid off. Besides, I wasn't too crazy about bein' no warehouseman either—just some asshole's gopher. Join the army and learn a fuckin' trade, man. All I did was shoot at people and smoke dope and try not to get my own ass shot off. Not much call for those trades in Sacramento, man.

Artie finds a newspaper in a garbage can, so we plant ourselves on a bus stop bench. T.J. grabs the sports, man, and Cleve looks at the front page. Artie digs the want ads.

"Can you believe all the jobs, man?" Artie asks. "And not one worth a fuck, unless you are a damn engineer or somethin'. Well, the kid's not sweatin' for no minimum wage. Not for the kid, thank you."

T.J. grunts, "The world sucks."

"Sheee', le's go knock some mothahfuckah on the head, get some mo' scratch," suggests Big Cleve.

"Go to jail," chants Artie. "Go directly to jail. Do not pass go. Do not collect $200."

"Ah, man...," says Cleve. "You scared of the damn pigs."

"You're not?" demands Artie.

"*Hell* no—me, a mothahfuckin' revolutionary, scared? Sheee'."

"That's what I always figured you was, man," I grinned.

"Hell yeah! I *be* into the revolution, bro', liberatin' all kinda trash. Chi-chi-chi!"

We're across the street from Milo's Laundromat, man, a place we sometimes pick up a little jingle, and I'm checkin' out everybody that goes in or out, lookin' for a mark, or some leg, for *somethin'*, man.

"Look at that little kid all dressed like a guy," T.J. grunts.

"Where, man?"

"Right there."

"Oh yeah," I say. This little guy in a suit and tie and a snappy hat, man, is waddlin' up the other side of the street, headin' toward us. He's got this big head. "Hey," I say, "that's not a kid. It's one of those midgets."

"Where?" asks Cleve, suddenly interested.

"Dwarf, man," points out Artie. "That guy is a dwarf, not a midget."

"You ever screw one a them?" T.J. asks Artie.

For a second, Artie looks real thoughtful. "The kid did one after the county fair in Modesto," he answers, "on a dare."

The fuckin' kid claims he screwed everything, man. He gives me the ass sometimes.

"I was in high school and I thought it'd be a trip. It was, little teeny legs and arms." He gets that thoughtful look again, and adds. "Had a regular-size box, though." T.J. and Cleve crack up.

"You too much, slick," says the big guy, then he glances away. "Look at that li'l dude," chuckles Cleve. "Chi-chi-chi!"

"All dressed up, man," I say, tired of fuckin' Artie's fuckin' stories. "Ready for a big time. Let's go hit on the dude."

We stroll across the street, man, and lean on the wall outside the laundromat. "My man clean," croons Cleve, "Chi-chi-chi!"

The small guy swaggers up the street, man. When he reaches us, Cleve calls in this soft voice: "Say, li'l dude. Wha's happenin'?"

The midget stops. He looks up at Cleve. The dude's got a regular size head, man, but the rest of him is all shrunk, and his clothes are miniature. I'm givin' the dude the eye, man, because I never seen a midget up close before. He notices me. "Kiss off, buster," he spits in this voice that sounds like his tape is playin' too fast.

The midget tries to walk around Cleve, but my man blocks his way. "Wha's the hurry, bro'?" asks Cleve grinnin'.

"I'm gonna call a cop on you bums," the little dude warns.

"Bums!" I say, givin' Cleve a big wink. "Hey, man, we're veterans!"

"Chi-chi-chi!"

Artie advises, "Let the guy go. He is not botherin' nobody."

"He bother *me*," Cleve says. You never know what might piss the big guy off. "Why he so clean and we wearin' rags?"

"The kid does not need any of this action. The kid does not need those orange coveralls," says Artie, and he recrosses the street and sits back down on the bench. T.J. ain't said nothin', man.

"What you think, T.?" asks Cleve.

T.J., that is always pissed, he growls. "I think the fucker's a smart-ass."

I can tell the little guy's gettin' pissed or scared or both, man, and I'm about to let him slide, but then he hisses at us, "Veterans! No wonder we couldn't whip a buncha slant-eyed gooks if creeps like you was in the army. Get outta my way!"

Cleve's eyes flare. He reaches down and scoops the little dude up—those stumpy arms and legs swingin' and kickin', that high voice howlin': "Help!"—and carries him into the laundromat. T.J. opens the glass door on a king-sized dryer. "Throw the fucker in here," he says, and Cleve does, T.J. snappin the round glass door shut.

These two old ladies that was sittin' by a washer, man, they scurry out the door while I fish for a quarter, then push it into the machine and watch the little smart-ass start to tumble, thumpin' against the sides and howlin' all the time, man. It's great. I lean back against a washin' machine to dig the show.

"Better'n T.V., bro'," says Cleve. "Chi-chi-chi!"

T.J. still sounds pissed, man. "Let the little fucker dance. That's probably what he was doin' while we was in Nam."

Through the sound of the dryer, I hear my name, so I turn around, man, and see Artie wavin'. I wave back and motion him to come over, man, but he shakes his head and points up the street real frantic. Fuck it, man. I turn back to watch the little dude dance, but no sooner'n I get settled than the pigs bust in.

Before I know what's happenin', I'm bent over the machine with my arms twisted behind my back and cuffs bein' snapped on. When the pigs straighten me up, man, the midget is out, leanin' against the front of the dryer, and he's almost cryin' he's so shook up. His face is purple, and he's screechin' while these two pigs try to calm him down. We ain't sayin' shit.

Finally, this old cop looks at us, man, and shakes his head. "What in God's name were you guys thinkin' about?" he asks. "You could've killed that guy. What goes on in your heads?"

"Fuck him," spits T.J., and I think to myself that it might not be exactly the right thing to say.

The pig's face hardens, his eyes narrow, man, and he looks at me and Cleve and T.J. "You're scum," he finally spits. "We need to bury scum like you in the joint so decent people can live."

"Nobody said we was scum when they sent us to Nam, man," I spits. "We was decent enough for that."

"We've gotta make the world safe for decent people, safe from your kind," the cop says, his voice real quiet and cold.

T.J. just glares back at him. "Your world sucks," he says.

Across the street, man, over the cop's shoulder and past the crowd of decent people gatherin' out on the sidewalk, pressin' their decent noses against the glass, man, I see Artie standin' by the bench. He's all alone, and he looks real lonely, man, like a kid that's just lost somethin'.

The Estero

THE ROAD CLIMBS AROUND A HILL WEST OF
Tomales, passing the old Catholic Cemetery, then border-
ing a steeply sloping pasture where a dairyman dumps
waste from his barn, where grass grows rapidly and dark all year
round. During summer when I was a kid I used to walk there and
examine the drainage ditch along the road beneath that slanted
field where muddy offal crusted and split into sharply geometric
designs. It always seemed vaguely magical to me.

A hundred yards farther southwest, the road crests and veers,
and a narrower lane intersects from the right. This one follows the
course of a brook and is densely lined by willows as it swoops down
the hill's other side, dropping to the eucalyptus border of my uncle's
farm where the small creek joins a much larger stream crossed by
a wooden bridge. In fact, that one-lane road actually separates our
house from our barn and corrals.

The land flattens beyond what we still call Uncle Tony's farm,

a wide valley opening into verdant fields dotted with dairy cows
and clusters of shaggy sheep. It is in a hidden vale surrounded by
rolling hills, one that tourists and even some locals never see. Even
if they *are* here, they usually forget that our place is only four miles
from the Pacific and little higher than sea-level. The larger stream
winding through our property—the Estero—reveals an oceanic
link and it too was a continual source of wonder to my sister Suzie
and me when we were small.

It is called the Estero, because its estuarial water ebbs and flows
with the tides. During wet winters, it can swirl muddy brown, but
most of the year it boasts no noticeable flow at all, only a tidal
pulsing; it is a sleepy, secret filament of the sea, its channel full
of dark water that reveals at unpredictable times the primal
surging of its source: vast phantom fish might bulge its surface,
gulls might clatter to feast on minnows, an errant sea lion might
appear midstream in our pasture amidst feeding cattle, large
brown astonished eyes meeting large brown astonished eyes.

One time when we were kids my sister and I were fishing from
the bridge when we noticed something surging up the Estero, a
wake without a boat and traveling fast. "Hey, look!" I called, and
it slid directly beneath us, a watery shadow that appeared as large
as a calf. After it passed, small waves lapped the shore for several
seconds. "What was *that*?" she asked.

"I think it was a big giant shark."

Suzie stared at me for a prolonged moment, then began crying.

While I was trying to quiet her, concerned that Uncle Tony
might think I'd committed some minor atrocity, old Manuel
Gomes, my uncle's only employee, wandered over with his dog
from the milking barn to see what was wrong. "Leetle one," he

assured my sister, "the beeg feesh no get you. He come up here for bath only." He grinned with his brown teeth and we both smiled. "Yeah, up north pasture een the beeg pool, meester feesh wash hees feens and seeng a feesh song: tra-la-la-la!" He rolled his eyes and his voice grew high and hollow. Then he grinned once more and, while his hard old hand stroked Suzie's dark hair, his dog nuzzled her, wagging its ebony tail. She giggled, shark forgotten.

Manuel was our favorite, mine and Suzie's. He had no family, only Shep—or "Shap" as he called him—not a shepherd at all despite his name, but a one-eyed black labrador who spent as much time in the Estero as he did on land. The man and his pooch lived in a small cabin on the strange stream's bank across the road near the milking barn. He had worked for my uncle since way before I was born, since right after coming over from The Azores, and Manuel had been no kid then, Tony told me. Like his dog, he loved the Estero.

"Een heem I catch salmons and beeg tunas weeth my peechfork," Manuel once told me, nodding toward that dark vein of water. Like most local farmers, he harvested the Estero without benefit of rod or reel. He also didn't seem to know one fish from another: his tuna might be a catfish or a carp. "And many leetle feeshes, herreengs and anchov's. And beeg sturgeons: Ugly! Son a the beetch! I catch heem many times. Juan Battancourt that works for Dolcini, he say he see beeg whale sweem by the cows. Son a the beetch! And weeth my own eyes I see the seals many times. Thees loco dog"—he nodded at Shep—"he theenk he ees one, a seal." He scratched the ebony head and, I swear, Shep showed his white teeth in a smile, his tail wagging.

One spring day when Suzie was off with our mother, Manuel took me down the Estero all the way to the sea. He had built an old boat that looked like a blunt, wooden canoe; it was barely large enough for Shep and the two of us, but we loaded it with lunch and shoved off just below his cabin and began slowly winding our way westward through lush pastures, sitting low on the current- less stream, high banks on both sides, our eyes at grass level. Cattle and sheep viewed us warily as we slid by below them. Every few minutes, it seemed, Manuel would say, "Loook at heem!"—and point at a garter snake slipping through the water, at a long heron spiking minnows, at a turtle plopping into the stream from a snag—"Son a the beetch!"

Above us and the estuarial pastures through which we traveled shrugged the hulking shoulders of coastal hills; as it neared the sea, the Estero sliced through increasingly steep country creating a deeper and narrower canyon. In places it appeared there could be no outlet, the hills folding so intimately, but an unexpected turn, a secret course, and the channel would bend on itself, slipping through to another small valley. As we approached the stream's mouth—not seeing or even hearing it, but smelling it in the strong, salty wind that resisted us, forcing both Manuel and me to paddle hard in order to make any progress—Shep grinned into that zephyr, pink tongue lolling.

Finally the Estero swung wide around a treeless bluff and I began hearing the dark rumblings of what seemed a distant surf. Only a moment later, to my surprise, we were gazing at the great blue Pacific bursting against the white sand of a small beach, at a churning expanse as open as freedom itself. It was low tide and the Estero appeared to be blocked by a sandbar, so it had formed

a small, shallow lake on the beach. We pulled the boat ashore—Shep splashing and romping in that estuarial pond—then ate our lunch on the steep sand just beyond cresting breakers. Shep chased shorebirds and the shells Manuel occasionally threw for him. When we were about to return, lunch consumed, tide rising, a sleek dark head popped from the frothing water directly in front of us and for a moment, I stared at a sea lion staring at me. Then it was gone. "Did you *see* that?" I asked.

"Son a the beetch! I see heem!" A moment later Shep was exploring the surf where the sea lion had appeared, his own sleek, dark head dipping under water, then popping up. "Loook, another seal!" laughed Manuel.

When the frustrated pooch finally emerged, we all climbed back into Manuel's small boat and paddled home, strong ocean gusts now pushing us, and Shep faced backward, still grinning, tongue still lolling into the wind. "Loook at Shap," said the old man with a wink. "Een hees dreams he ees a seal." Then he reached over and scratched his dog's glistening black head.

Manuel and I always intended to make that trip again, but never did. He grew older and I grew up. Shep-the-seal's snout and paws whitened. The old man and the old dog hobbled around the farm, both troubled by arthritis but both continuing their duties. They even looked alike, those two, Manuel's dark Portuguese complexion seeming to deepen as his hair whitened. Anyway, I finally finished my degree in husbandry at the university and returned to help Tony on the farm; since he had no other family, I was slated to eventually take it over.

Suzie was away at college when the deluge occurred. It wasn't, and isn't for that matter, uncommon for coastal streams engorged

with winter's heavy rain to flood these valleys, so that when storms clear, cattle wander through knee-deep water, feeding alongside egrets and gulls. But that year some of the highest tides on record coincided with heavy rains: a dangerous combination, since tides alone can overflow banks in these low-lying pastures. Combined they were more than we could imagine.

Uncle Tony, Manuel and I had sandbagged the cabin and the milking barn as a precaution, something we did virtually every winter. Our house sits on a hillock and had never been threatened by rising water. Then we had turned in, Manuel refusing to join us in the house: "Me and Shap no scare a the leetle rain. Son a the beetch!" He and his stoved-up old pooch had hobbled off to their lair and Uncle Tony had laughed, "He's a tough old bastard. Son a the beetch," he winked, and we both laughed.

When my uncle awoke the next morning about five, it was still dark and rain was pounding the roof. He usually allowed me to rise on my own, but that day he rousted me immediately. "Come look at this," he insisted.

He'd pulled on his clothes over the long-johns he slept in all winter, and I did the same. He walked me to the front porch and in the darkness I saw what looked like a dark, moving mirror. Water was lapping at the porch and our entire valley appeared full: one vast lake. "What the hell!" I grunted.

It was still dark and clouds hung heavily over us, but the rain had lightened to drizzle. "I never seen it like this before," my uncle said.

"Me either."

"We're gonna lose some stock for sure."

That's when I looked at him and said, "Manuel?"

"Oh, Jesus. Let's get the flashlights."

The cabin was gone, and by the time we waded to the barn——water chest-deep and cold, footing treacherous—located Tony's bass boat, then got the outboard motor started, darkness had begun lifting, replaced by an eerie luminescence as brown and murky as the water that surged around us. Clouds still rolled above us, and we didn't know for certain which way to go since water wasn't flowing downstream—it wasn't flowing at all, just curling, curling. The cabin wasn't visible in our valley, so I said, "Let's head for Dolcini's," and we did.

Tony pointed the boat's prow toward the coast and we headed west as rain once more increased. Near the bridge where Highway 1 crosses the Estero, we found the cabin wedged into a grove of eucalyptus, and Manuel was there clinging to its roof. While Tony held the boat steady, I managed to muscle the old man into it. He was stiff, his breath shallow and uneven, but he managed to gasp, "Where ees he, Shap?"

My eyes caught Tony's, but he shook his head. "We can't look for the dog," he said. "We've gotta get Manuel to the doctor. He's in rough shape."

"Where ees he?" the old man moaned over and over again as we rushed him toward Tomales where a doctor could treat him, then send him to the hospital in Santa Rosa. Tony accompanied Manuel but I returned home and took the bass boat back to Dolcini's just before dark: no luck. That night I telephoned all the nearby places that still had lines up, but we never found any trace of Shep.

The old bridge was gone—it ended up on our lower pasture—so there was only one route to and from town when the water

receded. We brought Manuel home in the pickup a week after the flood and moved him into our house. He did not speak no matter what we said to him, but after another day, he dressed and wandered from the house to the remains of the bridge where he stared at the brown water—tides were still running high—and spat into the stream.

He remained there most of that day, and most of the next one. When he limped in for supper, I asked, gently, how things were going. For a minute he gazed at me then away. I didn't really expect a reply, but he fooled me. "I see heem there, Shap, sweemeeng weeth the other seals. He ees happy."

I knew he couldn't have seen Shep but it didn't matter. "That's great, Manuel," I said.

He smiled. "Shap," he said.

The following day, we were still busy repairing damage done by the water, so my uncle and I didn't hover around Manuel, although we did try to keep an eye on him. But not a close enough one, for he somehow put his old canoe into the water and was paddling west when I noticed. Damn! Since I was in the process of pulling a mired cow from a bog with the tractor, I didn't need the added chore of chasing after him, but I had it. Tony was way to hell and gone up in the hills feeding hay to cattle on the upper slopes of our property, so there was no one else to pursue the old man.

By the time I got the bass boat started, Manuel and the canoe had disappeared. I knuckled the outboard down and roared off to catch him, but when I rounded that first bend I couldn't see his head moving over the pasture of the next wide valley as I had anticipated. A moment later, I knew why. I rounded another

serpentine curve and there was the canoe with the old man lying in it like some ancient warrior consigned to the sea. His breath rattled and his eyes were open and glazed. I took off my jacket and covered him, then began tethering the two boats but almost immediately the ragged breathing stopped. I checked Manuel for a pulse but there was none, so I reached over and placed his hat on his face, sighed, then finished attaching the tow-line to the canoe.

That accomplished, I sat for a moment before starting the engine, glancing from the old man's body, then at the pasture with winter grass flattened by the flood and at the hills ahead. I gazed away to the west where the Estero twisted toward the sea, and the stream's surface was suddenly broken by the sleek, black head of a surfacing sea lion. Within me tears began their hot surge, but my face remained dry all the way back to the farm.

That all happened when I was a kid. Now I'm hobbling around this place myself, with grandchildren visiting each summer and with a daughter and son-in-law planning to take over the dairy when I retire, which will be soon. It was a long time ago, but if you climb that road out of Tomales today to the old Catholic Cemetery you can find where Manuel's body rests. I was one of his pallbearers and we placed him there in our family plot next to my dad. Uncle Tony's with him now, and my mother, and my wife. And that's where my bones will rest one day soon.

But Shep isn't there. He's at sea with the other seals, and I'm sure that Manuel's spirit is with him. And mine, my spirit is traveling its own Estero, swimming toward Shep and Manuel and the freedom of that secret sea beyond hills or memories or the salty wind of coastal canyons.

The Attack of The Great Brandy Bear

"H EY DAD," MY BOY CRAIG HE CALLED, "wasn't it last summer they had that big party down at the ranger station?"

It took me a second to catch on, what with bein' semi-winded and all, then I said, "Yeah it was, just about a year ago, I reckon."

Earl and Bob Don and Big Dunc they never took the bait—too pooped—so Craig he give it another try. "I've never seen so many kegs of beer, and the bands . . ."

Bob Don he finally nibbled. "Bands, way up here in Tuolomne Meadows?" he asked.

"Yeah," grinned Craig, his braces glitterin', "they were celebrating the first time a backpack party ever made it over this trail without at least one guy getting mauled by a bear." I winked at my kid that's about half-sharp for a thirteen-year-old if I do say so myself.

The boys they never said nothin' and I seen Big Dunc look at

40

Earl real funny, like he just nibbled a turd by mistake. Finally, Bob Don, that's pretty quick hisself, havin' graduated Bakersfield Junior College and all, he said with this teensy smile, "Well, at least we know it *can* be done." Duncan and Earl never laughed.

There we took a blow under pine trees next to Cathedral Creek, a long ways from the nearest bar stool, and the boys they was out of their element. Them three was greenhorns and not exactly the outdoor types. Ol' Dunc he carried a bigger pack hangin' over his belt buckle than he did on his back, and his Yukon Jack t-shirt it'd been soaked with sweat before we'd walked a hundred yards. How come us to be alongside that Sierra trail is a story itself.

See, us boys we'd been settin' around the Tejon Club back in Oildale sippin' beer one afternoon about a month before and ol' Wylie Hillis 'uz givin' one a his stories: "Me and Myrtle had drove up this mountain road," he said all serious, "which it was a real desolate deal. Anyways, whenever we stopped to eat sandwiches, a gi'nt grizzly bear it come out from the woods and made for us! Let me tell ya, boys, we skedaddled!"

"Oh bullshit, Wylie," I said. "I been hikin' them Sierras for years and I never seen a bear chase no one."

"Well you been missin' somethin', bud," he snapped right back.

Bob Don that reads all the time, he chuckled then explained just as patient as could be, "Wylie, there aren't any grizzlies left in the Sierra Nevadas. The last one was shot at Horse Corral Meadows in 1921."

You'd think that'd shut the old coot up, but no. "Me and the missus seen one, perfesser," he snorted. He was real jealous of Bob Don's education.

Bob Don he just shook his head.

"I heard them grizzly bears're bad," said Earl that runs the joint.

"Well, I been backpackin' for twenty years and I never had no trouble with bears," I told him, which it was true, too. I seen plenty bruins and lost a little food, but I never had no fuss with 'em. "About the only time those bears can be a problem is if you run into a sow with cubs, then she might attack if she figgers you to be a threat. And even then, not grizzlies, only black bears."

"I tell ya, Dan'l Boone," Wylie, that's never backpacked a step in his life, he said to me real sarcastic, "you and yer scouts there give 'er a try this year 'cause them grizzlies're back 'cause me and Myrtle we seen one." He dipped his chin real strong on that last word, then off he walked in a huff—full of shit like always.

Anyways, that's what got me and the boys to talkin' about backpackin'. Before long, while the brew it kept flowin' purty good and our tongues got real loose, Earl and Bob Don an' Big Dunc they decided that they oughta give it a try—"Shit, if Jerry Bill can do that packin' deal *anybody* can," Dunc winked at the others—and we agreed to take us a week off and hit for the hills.

"Me, I always wanted to try that stuff," said Earl.

"Hell yeah," Big Dunc conceded, "I'uz the best hiker in my outfit back in the army." He 'uz the best ever'thing back when he'uz in the army, accordin' to him.

"I'm for it," agreed Bob Don.

So my boy Craig and me we planned it out, choosin' this real gentle trail that run from Tuolomne Meadows down to Yosemite Valley. Heddy, my wife that's a school teacher, she advised, "You'd *better* choose an easy route because you're apt to have to carry Big Drunk most of the way." She talks funny like that—and so does Craig, for that matter—but she's a hell of gal, Heddy.

"That's Big Dunc," I corrected.

But it turned out Heddy she was right. Here we was, just startin' out really, and Duncan already looked like he'd been shot at and missed but shit at and hit. He plopped there like a road apple next to the trail with them other two whenever Craig took to kiddin' 'em. Wasn't none of 'em lookin' too good. "What do ya think, boys?" I finally called. "Time to hit that trail again?"

"Whyn't we just camp here," Dunc urged.

"Yeah," agreed Earl.

Bob Don that was taking a long pull from his canteen, he nodded.

"We ain't come but about a mile, boys," I pointed out. "At this rate we won't make Yosemite Valley before Christmas...a next year. We need to put in two or three more miles—at least get to the top of this pull. It's basically all downhill from there." Not exactly true, but close.

"It'll be easier once we reach the top," Craig agreed.

"This deal couldn't *git* no harder," gasped Duncan.

Out the corner of his mouth, Craig he whispered to me: "I think Big Drunk is out of shape."

"That's Big Dunc," I corrected, then I turned to the boys. "Listen," I said, "I warned you guys not to split that six-pack this mornin' before we left."

"Hey, it's vacation, ain't it?" Earl interrupted.

Yeah, it's vacation, but beer don't go too good with hikin'. But at the rate you three're sweatin', that beer'll be gone dir'ctly and you'll take to feelin' better."

"Cain't feel no worse," grunted Dunc.

Two hours later we'd managed another mile or so. We'uz

plopped next to this boggy little meadow where the trail forked to Cathedral Lakes. "This is the life," Bob Don said in the voice of a man confessin' murder. Earl he'd just downed a couple more aspirins and Dunc—between gasps—he was tellin' Craig how he used to grab rattlesnakes by their tails and snap their heads off whenever he'uz a kid back in Texas. "Really?" said Craig, downright impressed.

Just then Bob Don let out a war hoop—"Eeek!"—and rose straight off the ground like a damn helicopter. "Snake!" he screamed. "Snake!"

"Where at?" I asked and Earl, that's already on his feet, pointed a quiverin' finger at a little dark ribbon 'bout the size of a night crawler that's crossing the trail beside us.

"Snap his head off, Mr. Duncan," called Craig, winkin' at me. "Mr. Duncan?"

Well, Mr. Duncan he wasn't no place to be seen. He'd cut a new trail straight up the hillside with Bob Don closin' on him. Them guys could sure motor, tired as they was. My boy he shook his head and grinned, then he picked the little garter snake up—it curlin' right away around his hand like they do—and he stroked its tiny head. Earl backed way off. "I think I'll show this to Big Drunk when he gets back," Craig said.

"That's *Dunc,*" I insisted. I never wanted him gettin' *Mr. Duncan,* that's semi-hot headed, sore at me.

We finally made camp a hour or so later next to a boulder on this little flat beside another small creek. There was this big rock outcroppin' to shield us from the evenin' breeze. Craig helped the boys set up our two-man tent, which all the three of 'em intended

to sleep in. Me and Craig we figured to roll our bags and pads out on a ground cloth.

I'd set up my little Bluet stove and was cookin' freeze-dried chili. I had water boilin' over a campfire for instant soup and I'd already went and mixed some instant butterscotch puddin' for dessert. "What's that, baby shit?" asked Earl, a beer-nut and pickled-egg gourmet as well as a mountain man. "Ain't you got no steaks?"

Just then, from around the rock come Big Dunc and Bob Don. They carried four metal cups fulla snow they'd gathered from a small drift just up the hill. "Time for snow cones," said Bob Don. He opened the pack he'd rented in Bakersfield and produced a quart bottle of brandy.

"Hey," I said, "I told you guys no booze up here."

"You also said we could have anything we could carry," asserted Bob Don.

"Yeah," I added, "and I'm carryin' *your* food because *you* said *your* pack was too heavy."

"Shut up and pour," Dunc said to Bob Don. He did, placin' my brandy next to me on a rock. I determined to just let the damn thing sit there. Except that a minute later, I reached down and took me just a teeny little sip. Then I took another'n. In fact, I emptied mine just about as fast as they did theirs, and had a couple more. It sure tasted good, and by supper time we's havin' one hell of a party, laughin' and carryin' on. Craig he come back from fishin' in the creek with four little trout and said, "I heard you guys way upstream."

I give him a slap on the back and grinned, "Wrap them trout in foil with a little butter in their bellies and we'll give these here greenhorns a treat." I'uz feelin' flat loose by then.

Smack! A damn snowball caught me on the neck and near made me spill my brandy. That skinny Bob Don had snuck off and filled an empty food bag with snow while we figgered he's takin' a leak, and he's on the attack. Well, we battled for a while, Craig in the middle of it, chuggin' over to that snow drift for ammo, and the fight woulda went on longer but 'cept Earl caught Big Drunk in the nuts with snow glob, and Duncan right away got pissed. We cooled him off with another brandy snow cone.

It'uz dark by the time we et, and I'uz drunker'n a dancin' cootie. Must a been the damn altitude, but that brandy helped too. After dinner ol' Craig he washed the dishes and I tied our food up in a tree just in case a hungry bruin happened by—about three foot off the ground is all I managed with Craig laughin' at me—then I crawled into my down bag on the ground cloth next to Craig's and commenced snorin'. The three muskrateers they somehow sardined into that teeny tent.

"HEYYYYY!" That scream by the trio it woke me right up. I heard one hell of a commotion and seen three flashlight beams pop on from where the tent was set up. "Bear! Bear! Bear!" come the voices. I'uz a little confused, my head it ached, and my mouth tasted like toad turds, but I followed them light beams and, sure enough, the bag a food it was gone from the tree: just the rope swingin' there, three foot off the ground.

"A grizzly went and got the food deal," I heard Dunc accuse, his voice quiverin'. "You said there *wasn't* no bears!"

"You shoulda seen 'im, a gi'nt damn grizzly," moaned Earl.

"It was! It really was," Bob Don gasped.

"Huh," I said. Then, "Well, it's gone now. Go to sleep. We'll look for it in the mornin'. I'd been in them mountains enough to

know that a bear'll just eat what it can and throw the rest around, and that it wouldn't be comin' back, so I rolled over just as Craig snuck back into his bag.

After a second, it dawned on me: "You little devil," I whispered, "what'd you go and do?"

"I just gave your friends a thrill," he giggled.

I shook my head, laughed, then went back to sleep.

It was comin' light but the sun wasn't up yet whenever I heard Earl call: "I gotta pee somethin' fierce. You reckon it's safe?"

I opened my blinkers and there set them three woodsmen with their faces huddled against the mosquito net door a that little tent, eyes lookin' like they'd been blow-torched. I bet they never slept since the big bear attack. Craig he'uz sawin' logs next to me.

"Dunc can go with you for a guard," I answered.

"No way," shot the big guy. "No way in hell."

"He's already peed his own pants," Earl added. I don't think he was kiddin'.

Oh well, I needed me two aspirins anyways, so I climbed outta my fart sack and got a fire started while them three little orphans they huddled there in the tent. Finally, Earl he inched out and walked two whole steps before he drained his radiator, lookin' around all the time like he's expectin' a attack. "Hey, you're splattering us," complained Bob Don.

Me, I wandered around that big boulder we'd built our campfire against, and found the food where Craig'd stashed it, then come back and fixed the coffee. Truth is, I coulda used a couple beers to shut down that jackhammer in my head, then used that jackhammer to knock the skunk shit off my teeth: my mouth was bad.

"You should've seen that bear," said Bob Don that finally got up enough courage to crawl out from the tent and join me. His eyes they looked like pee holes in snow.

"Yeah," I grinned. They never did catch on.

We was a couple miles down the trail that mornin' after eatin' whenever I suggested that we shed our packs and hike up this little peak right close so they could see the view. It wasn't much of a climb at all and you could see from heck to breakfast from there. For the boys it was a tough decision: they sure as hell wanted to drop them packs—and the big clubs each one of 'em toted to fight off grizzlies—but they never wanted to walk uphill. They never wanted to walk a-tall. Finally, I convinced 'em and we leaned our gear against these trees and took off across country to that low summit.

Me and Craig we was the first ones back and, whenever we got there, our packs had been knocked all over the hell and tore open. A damn bear had went and busted into 'em and got our food, spreadin' foil and plastic and chunks a this 'n' that all over, and in broad daylight too. I couldn't hardly believe it. I'd never had nothin' like that happen to me before.

Course the bear itself wasn't nowheres to be seen. It'd did its damage and took off, so me and Craig we scouted around to pick up whatever grub we could salvage, not worryin' too much about whether the bruin had chewed it a little or not. Them's our eats, and I for one wasn't goin' hungry because of a little bear spit.

Craig, he got our little camp stove started and boiled some water for tea. We had to decide if we'd salvaged enough food to go on or if we had to head back the way we come. The boys, meanwhile, was givin' me seven kinds a hell.

"Oh no," wailed Big Dunc that by then had a club in *each* hand, "there ain't no bears in these mountains. Hell, ol' Wylie he was right on that deal." His head it was swivelin' around like he's watchin' a damn tennis game.

"You're one hell of a guide, Jerry Bill," Earl said to me. "You brung us straight into bear couuntry. Hell's bells!"

Bob Don he set there with his club on his lap and he shook his head. "It's *uncanny*," he said.

"Uncanny?" I smiled, but Bob Don wasn't tryin' to be funny.

"That we'd run into all these bears," he continued.

"I told you," smirked Craig that wasn't too worried.

"Yeah," Duncan nodded, "there's a lot more to this packin' deal than I figgered."

"There sure as hell is," agreed Earl.

"Well," I told 'em, "you might come up here ever'day for a year and not see another bear, so just relax. Me and Craig we come up ever' summer and this's never happened before."

After I give the boys some tea and that nice Sierra sun it warmed 'em up a tad, they calmed down. I fixed us each a cup a bear-slobber stew and nobody complained much mainly because it was that or nothin'. Big Dunc said he could sure use a beer— or a brandy—and we all laughed.

With everybody feelin' good again, I excused myself real polite and scuttled downslope into this little gulley so's I could heed nature's call, as they say. I'uz makin' for this big huge hemlock about a hundred foot below where our gang set. Whenever I got there, I smelled bear—like a real strong kennel—that I'd sniffed a few times before. I forgot my business and commenced sniffin'

around and, sure as hell, right in that tree's thick branches I seen the shape of a good-sized bruin outlined by sunlight.

I picked a different tree for my bathroom, then I climbed back up to the trail and said to Craig, "See that big hemlock down there?"

"Yeah?"

"Well, our friend the bear's takin' a little siesta under it."

"Really?" he asked, then he walked toward it and took a look for himself.

"You be careful," I cautioned him.

"Where 's he goin'?" demanded Duncan.

I debated about how to answer, but finally figgered what the hell. "There's a bear snoozin' under that tree. Craig just went to take a peak."

"No shit?"

"No shit. Wanta go have a look?"

"Hell no!"

"A bear? Where?" demanded Earl, his club at the ready.

Bob Don he shook his head real glum. "Not another one."

"It's *uncanny*," I said. I liked that word. Then I noticed Dunc struggle to his feet and commence hoofin' down the trail, no pack or nothin'.

"Where're you goin'?" I called.

He never answered, so Earl and Bob Don they hollered at him too. We musta woke up that bruin 'cause just about then a cinnamon-colored bear with two cubs sorta lurched out from the cover of that hemlock and stood blinkin' her little bitty eyes, them two cub no bigger'n a minute and cute as could be. Even then Bob Don and Earl, that was strugglin' to pull their packs on, they was

still with us. But whenever I asked Craig, "You reckon ol' momma there's lookin' for another snack?" and he pegged a rock at that sow to chase her off, well the boys they retreated, hot on Dunc's heels.

Funny thing is that the trail it turned a hairpin around the edge a the canyon, so whenever Mrs. Bear and her babies crashed away from us, they went straight across through the trees and on up the other side until they crossed that very same path—about five foot in fronta Duncan. He hit the brakes hollerin', "They got us surrounded!" Then he barreled right back, knockin' Bob Don and Earl ass over teakettle, then them two tried to scramble up, wrestlin' each other to get away from that man-eater—that had long-since disappeared upslope with her cubs.

Well, it took awhile, but we finally got a shiverin' Duncan to shoulder his own pack and we tippy-toed the mountaineers back down the trail to the car, me havin' to send Craig ahead to scout and guarantee that there wasn't no ambush. Craig he figgered it's the most fun he ever had outside a Disneyland, and I enjoyed it too, I gotta admit, but Earl and Bob Don and Big Drunk they looked like they coulda found somethin' they appreciated more.

They cheered whenever we reached the trailhead and our car, them three muskrateers, then they conked out just as soon as we took off for home, curled in the backseat snorin' ever'one. Just before we arrived back in Oildale, Earl he woke up and said real sleepy, "Drop me by the club, willya? I'll buy you guys a beer. Craig, you get a coke."

So we stopped at the Tejon Club and ever'one piled out and hit for the bar. Who was settin' there big as life but ol' Wylie Hillis.

"Looky here," he called, "the campers're back. Never took you boys long, did it?"

"Naw," I smiled, "we moved right along."

"It'uz a rough deal," I heard Duncan growl under his breath.

"See any bears?"

Nobody answered for a minute, then Craig he said real innocent, "Yeah, just a few. We chased them away from our food, didn't we Mr. Duncan?"

Mr. Duncan'uz up to his ears in a beer mug, so he snorted, "What's that? Oh yeah. Damn rights! Pegged rocks at 'em is what we done."

"Is that a fact?" gasped Wylie.

Big Dunc'uz gettin' braver as he went along. "Damn rights! One of 'em she had two babies, but we run her off."

"Them're supposed to be real rough," pointed out Wylie.

"Not if you know how to handle 'em," Bob Don he asserted real firm.

"Was they grizzlies?"

"You damn rights!" Earl told him.

"I'll be go to hell," said Wylie, "and you boys run 'em off?"

"We sure as hell did," Duncan nodded, then he took another long pull from his beer.

"Bring Craig here another coke on me," Mr. Duncan he told the bartender.

"And that ain't all," Dunc slurred, "you shoulda seen the size a that rattlesnake I damn near grabbed and snapped the head off of."

Wylie whistled through his teeth, "Is *that* a fact?"

"Yessir," conceded Duncan, "it ain't nothing like a campin' deal

out in the fresh air." He ordered a fresh beer—his fourth in a hurry—and he'uz already semi-shit-faced.

"Nothin' like a little hike," agreed Earl.

"Right," grinned Bob Don that was lookin' a little tight his own self.

Craig, that was settin' next to me, he whispered, "They really had fun didn't they Dad? Especially Big Drunk."

"Big Drunk's the best outdoorsman in the world as long as he's settin' at this bar," I whispered back. "I reckon we oughta head for home before he commences wrestlin' that grizzly. We might could save the bear's life if we take right off."

Craig liked to fell off his stool laughin'.

Just as we hit the door, Big Drunk he said real jovial, "One thing, though—next time *I'm* tyin' the food deal up in a tree so's them damn grizzlies cain't git at it." Earl and Bob Don they both laughed.

Me, I just smiled and said, "I 'preciate all the help I can get." Craig and me we slid out the door and went home.

Blackness

DURING THAT THIRD WEEK BERNARD
Solomon's depression suddenly lifted. He had arisen
reluctantly in the middle of an afternoon, then slouched
into a shower where hot water eased his taut neck. Emerging, he
grabbed a towel and walked out of the steam-filled bathroom to
dry himself in his bedroom.

As he stood naked before the full-length mirror something
caught his eye, staring brightly back at him from the middle of his
chest, a tiny dark spot no larger than a pin's point. Solly moved
closer to the glass and examined the spot carefully. He tried to rub
it off, but it did not move. Like a speck of coal, glistening, it
remained there, attached to him, part of him, and it was black,
absolutely black.

He flopped back onto his bed, a silly smile suddenly slicing his
face. Could it be true? Was he finally turning black? Springing up,
he once more examined himself closely in the mirror and it was

there, the spot, black and absolutely real. He once more flopped grinning to the bed, nonetheless shaking his head. Had that last brutal episode been his crucible?

Even this new joy could not totally erase the scar of grinding humiliation he had suffered at the university. It had not really been his fault, he knew, since the English Department had advertised for a specialist in Black Literature, not a black specialist in literature, a distinction its members chose to ignore when persecuting him. Solly had at no time claimed to be *ethnically* black. His was, if anything, an error of omission. When he'd realized that the obsequious if hippocritical members of the hiring committee had assumed he was black—"...after all, who but a blackamoor," he had heard the chairman chuckle pompously to a colleague, "would squander a perfectly good Ph.D. program on a subject as marginal as Afro-American Literature?"—Solly had said nothing to correct their collective illusion.

True, he had invested much of his savings for cosmetic surgery to blunt his shark-fin nose, and he regularly had his hair Afroed at a downtown parlor. Yes, he carried himself—leaning, standing, walking—as he had seen street brothers posture themselves. And his idiolect, his very voice, was now unmistakably black. All these were cited by the English Department as evidence of his deception, but what they did not understand is that he did those things for *himself*, not for them. They had merely observed, then drawn false inferences.

How could they understand? Let each of them grow up the son of a Jewish shopkeeper in a black neighborhood. Let them be the klutz who couldn't dribble with his left hand or hit a fall-away jumper. Let them never learn to chicken properly and screw up

the dozens every time they tried to play. Let it be their booty that
got burned every time booty-on-the-boards was the game. He had,
in fact, been the neighborhood symbol of white inadequacies at
the very time recognition of the strengths within Afro-America
grew in him. Negroes had something to live for because they were
still fighting their version of Egyptian bondage, while Jews had
long since become Egyptians themselves. Let the committee face
those realities before judging him.

What the Dean, the Department Chairman, and the Affirmative Action Coordinator all ignored when they confronted him
was that he had made no effort to fool them. But there was
another, even more important point, one that Solly had chosen
to argue in his own defense: He *was* black in the deepest spiritual
sense, had willed himself black, chosen to accept its burdens and
its joys.

None of them understood, and the Affirmative Action Coordinator, whom Solly recognized as a classic oreo, had snarled at
him: "Knock off the *bullll*shit, man."

Although many students had praised his classes and some had
actually mounted a small demonstration in his behalf, even
though some strong faculty support for him developed around the
issue of academic freedom, college authorities had nonetheless
fired him in a particularly humiliating way, reading him off the
roster at a stormy general-faculty meeting. They did everything
but tear off his buttons and epaulets, then snap his red pencil.

Solly had retreated to bed, curling for nearly three weeks in a
drugged semi-sleep, arising only to snack, to relieve himself, and
to occasionally melt tension under a hot shower. In his despair,
it had never occurred to him that his undeniable spiritual

blackness could one day become so powerful that it would manifest itself physically. He'd not even dared to hope for such affirmation.

Examining the black spot, he once more rubbed it, making certain once more that it was real. He had trouble not touching it, not returning to the mirror to once more reexamine this sudden vision of his inner being. It was real, so he telephoned Boudroux and Greene, his main men, and happily suggested they hit a couple clubs that night, have a little taste, maybe score some sisters, *get down* in general. Boudroux jumped on it and so did Greene, but only after he'd asked Solly where he'd been hiding. Solomon said he'd been ill, then let it slide.

Dressed in his uptown best—alligator kicks, pocketless trousers, tight silk shirt open to show his tiny black spot plus gold, chains and chains of gold around his neck—Solly dazzled even his partners. "My man clean to-*night,* Jim," crooned Boudroux, "clean like a mothahfuckah!"

Greene, who had the bad habit of saying things before thinking them out, observed, "Are you *baaad* to-night or what, breeze. Sheee-it, we gon' have to check the bottom of yo' feet to see if you one a them or one a us." The two black men had cackled at Greene's remark, but it had stung Solly, who resented even the joking suggestion he could possibly be one of *them.*

His friend had simply not raised his consciousness to a point that allowed him to fully comprehend Solomon. There remained in Greene—in both of them, really—some of the same kind of insensitivity that had prompted younger street brothers to so mercilessly hassle Solly when he had first moved into the Fillmore District, even to rough him up once before Boudroux and Greene,

both of whom were bad dudes, had made believers of the young bloods. Those kids had seen him only as a white dude, and he realized that, at times, even his two main men didn't really understand who and what he was.

His spot had grown considerably, taking on the form of a small, ebony egg, when Arletha Spencer, his special fox, had recoiled from it. "Solly, baby," she'd gasped, "somethin's wrong with that thing. It's growin', like it's, you know, alive. You better go see you a doctor."

"What you mean, baby?"

"Look at it. It's growin' fast."

"Course it's growin'," he acknowledged, tempted to share his secret with her.

"You go down to the clinic," Arletha advised. "That thing's *nasty*."

"Nasty!" exploded Solomon, the word suddenly pushing him out of control. "Looky here, bitch, that spot *black*! Black as Mother Africa! *Nasty* my ass!"

"Your ass *white*," Arletha'd snapped in response. She didn't back down from anyone, and that conversation had alerted Solly to the trouble that soon led to their breakup. He sensed not only that she couldn't grow with him but also that she would never admit it.

Shortly after he'd split with Arletha, he had gone swimming at the Y with Greene. In the locker room, the black man had eyed Solly's spot for an uncomfortable length of time before asking how long it had been growing. When Solly told him, Greene, who worked as a medical technician and often assumed the air of a physician, clucked, "Check it out with your doc, breeze. You don'

want no shit like that growin' on you." Solly's reply had been noncommittal, but within himself he'd registered Greene's remark, thought about it, and had begun to see the pattern emerging.

Everything clarified when, a couple of weeks later, Solomon and Boudroux were changing in the Y's locker room and the black man had pointed at the spot and asked, "What *is* that?' Suddenly Solly understood. Brothers and sisters were in on it too, the conspiracy. From whites he had expected resistance, but it was Arletha and Greene and Boudroux who most deviously sought to deny his blackness. He was no longer fooled by their glib friendship. They had tolerated all the symbols that had so troubled his family—the kicks, the threads, the jive—but when his new black reality confronted them, they instinctively resisted.

They, Solly began to understand, were the real whites, just as he was the real black. They had opted for whiteness while he had chosen blackness and they had all met halfway. Well, he was moving on, into a new circle of friends, abandoning his old ones, determined this time not to allow his secret even to be suspected.

His crucial error came when he applied for a city job. Required to take a physical, he casually visited the assigned clinic and breezed through preliminaries. Only when Solomon removed his shirt did the young, black physician gasp and blink. Immediately he touched Solly's spot, which had developed an agreeable itch as it expanded. Regaining his composure, the doctor asked, "How long has this...ah...mole been here?" Alert, unwilling to be tricked, Solly replied, gauging the black man's agitation all the while.

"Uhmmm," muttered the physician, who scribbled on a note

pad, then tore off a sheet and handed it to Solomon. "If you'll take this down to Surgery, they'll remove that lesion for biopsy," he explained.

"Remove it! What you talkin' 'bout, man?" demanded Solly, who had expected that very suggestion from the moment the black man had seen the spot. "Who say I want it removed?"

The young physician seemed momentarily stunned, but quickly recovered. "Look, Mr. Solomon, that spot displays characteristics of a particularly dangerous form of skin cancer. Probably it's nothing, but if there's even a small chance that it's malignant, it's better to remove you from it, then put it in a bottle for the pathologist. You, we leave out of the bottle." He smiled at his own clever way of explaining matters, but Solly was not fooled.

"No."

The doctor appeared not to comprehend. "No?" he asked.

"No," repeated Solomon.

Perplexed, the young physician tried to reason once more: "Don't you understand that your life might be in danger?"

Solly understood too well that his life, his inner, his secret, his *real* life, was in danger from those who could not allow him to achieve the blackness for which he had suffered. The black man in the white coat hurriedly left him in the examination room but, before Solomon could dress and depart, returned with a middle-aged white woman whom he introduced as a surgeon. Now they're revealing themselves, Solly realized.

"What is this, Bernard," demanded the white surgeon in what he recognized as a bold, Jewish-mother attempt to cow him, "suicide? You don't understand what Dr. Dixon has been telling you? This lesion looks dangerously like melanoma. Let's get it off

you so we can have its pathology confirmed then begin any necessary therapy."

She was difficult to resist. The very familiarity of her approach forced Solly to retreat, but he finally managed to talk her into a compromise, amazed all the while at how she made him feel it was *her* body to which he was denying her access. Even after she had carved a tiny slice from his blackness, she did not hide her disappointment, her disgust, and Solly had gratefully escaped the clinic.

He would be called as soon as a pathologist's report was complete, no later than tomorrow afternoon. If the lesion was malignant, they'd want him to visit an oncologist right away, so keep his time open. Hell yeah, Solly thought, I'll just rush right back so you can finish the job. Don't hold your mothah fuckin' breath.

On the edge of panic, he scurried to his room and packed his shoulder bag. He had to hurry and he had to travel light, because the enormity of the conspiracy had become clear to him at the clinic. Even public agencies were involved and those physicians, with their white smocks and white minds, were the executioners. He escaped into the comfort of growing night toward a world he knew authorities never penetrated except in sealed squad cars. If he could be safe anywhere, it was there.

Some stares at first greeted him, but when he spoke they understood, his brothers and sisters heard the tortured rhythm of his speech, read the desperation in his eyes, and they knew he was soul. "You on the fly, bro'?" asked one pale cat.

"You got it, blood," replied Solly with fatigued frankness. "They closin' in."

The pale cat, whose hair was wrapped in a maroon kerchief, led Solly to a dark basement, relieved him of his cash, then brought him a bowl of greens cooked with greasy pork. To Solly, fatigued and famished, it tasted ambrosial. After eating, he fell into a deep, relieved sleep.

Laughing voices awakened him, and he eased one eye open, panning the room until he settled on three black men seated at the same small table where he had eaten. These were street brothers, not the shuck-and-jive-types who had befriended him at the university. These were, in fact, older, harder-looking versions of the dudes who had so hassled him when he'd moved into the Fillmore. A knot of apprehension curled in Solly, but he thrust it away and sat up. The three men eyed him and, for what seemed a long time, no one spoke, then the darkest and roughest-looking of the trio grinned tightly. "Say, niggah," he crooned, "you wan' play a little whis'?"

Only first names had been exchanged—Lee, Cabrini, and Shank, the others were called—because all were on the run and they didn't want to know exactly who their companions in the safe-house were. They shared the barren basement, receiving food delivered by the fair-skinned dude twice each day. No queries about how long any of them would be staying were ever made— none of them knew, or admitted knowing anyway—and no one hassled for money. When, at night, the four of them foraged dark streets for vulnerable whites, they always split what they gathered with the pale cat, who asked no questions.

Perhaps it was the richness of the food, but Solly was troubled by abdominal pain from his first night in the basement. He initially tried antacids, but they didn't help. Aspirin, in combina-

tion with antacids, offered some relief, but he just didn't feel right. Nonetheless, this desperate, almost delirious existence buoyed Solomon, who could ignore trivialities in the face of his first unquestioned acceptance for what he was, a brother.

Exactly three weeks after he'd fled into the heart of the ghetto, he collapsed while sprinting away from a howling burglar alarm, pulling hard to stay with his partners, when something popped in his middle. He slowed, then halted, looking with lover's longing at the three men disappearing around a corner, remembering the cackling card games, the tight talk about leg, the coke they'd snorted, and the rough jobs where his brothers had flashed to his aid. "All right, blood," he mumbled as he slowly slid down the wall against which he leaned and lost consciousness.

Squeezing back toward wakefulness in a brightly lit room, Solomon sensed immediately that sedatives were numbing and slowing his reactions. Be careful, he reminded himself. Then he visually searched the white room, moving only his eyes because he was uncertain how much more of himself he *could* move. It was what he'd expected, a hospital ward. Slowly, he explored his body: toes functioned, so did his fingers—so far, so good. A bit more confident, he bent elbows and knees, noting then a corresponding pain in his middle with each exertion. Ceasing all effort, Solly contemplated the vague ache. Now that he knew its location, sensing it lightly with each breath.

From his chest to his navel, he thought. From his...spot to his navel. Struggling to sit up and examine himself, he was leveled by a great scream of pain. God! Gasping, mind racing, he struggled to think things out. From his spot to his navel, why had they cut there? Why not just carve the spot off? Another question

bloomed: Why had the spot grown there anyway, in that particular place, over his heart?

The white people who ran the white hospital hadn't settled for excising his visible blackness. No, they had entered him like thieves ransacking a temple because they had figured out that the spot was only the outward sign of his inner metamorphosis. They had not only dug out his visible blackness, but they had also pillaged his body in search of his soul because they had guessed the truth about the spot's meaning.

A nurse emerged, wraith-like, from one side. "Mr. Solomon," she inquired, "are you alright?" He said nothing.

Another white form materialized and Solly's wrist was lifted and held, his brow was cupped by a cool palm, then the white form muttered something to the nurse, who drifted quickly away, returned, and slipped a slender needle into Solomon's unresisting arm.

These were the forces that had destroyed his spot, had excavated for his soul, and Solly was determined to give them no indication whether or not they had succeeded. In truth, he was not certain himself.

Slack, yet alert in spite of the overwhelming fatigue that sought to slowly swallow him, Solomon sensed a tiny nudge, a movement within his core like a small, secret animal alerting him, only him, of its hiding place. He knew then that the whites had not found it. All the doctors with all their equipment had been denied his innermost enigma.

He could at last relax for he felt it moving cautiously yet certainly within him, already beginning to fill the places they had

emptied, growing as his spot had grown, and moving him ever closer toward blackness, delicious blackness, blackness.

Upstream

for João Guimarães Rosa

THAT MORNING WHEN MY UNCLE ARLO EPS stalked out from the cabin buck naked, he declared, "I'm a unsheathed soul!" Then he dove right into the Kern River and swam, angling kinda upstream to fight the current so that, whenever he finally turned directly into it, he just hung in that swift water, about halfway across, straight out from where I stood watching him.

"An unsheathed soul?" I asked myself. That sounded more like some preacher than my uncle.

He sure picked a terrible place to swim, the river right there, just below where Kern Canyon opened into the Southern Sierras, because that water it was snow melt straight from the high country, and it come down fast and freezing. Directly above where Arlo took to swimming, there was these rapids couldn't no boat get through and, at the canyon's mouth, this cataract was boiling.

At first I just stood there and watched him, stunned I guess. Once Uncle Arlo got turned into the current, though, and chugged into a rhythm that held him even with me—slipping back, then pulling forward again—I hollered at him, "Uncle Arlo! Uncle Arlo!"

"Leave the ol' fool be," snapped Aunt Mazie Bee leaning on the dark cabin's doorway. "He's just a-tryin' to attract attention." She disappeared back into darkness talking to herself.

Me, I spent most of that morning watching my uncle surge, slip back, then surge again, as he tried to hold even with the cabin. You know, I'd never even seen him naked before, let alone acting so crazy, so I didn't know what to do. A couple times I asked Mazie Bee if we shouldn't try to help him some way.

"Help him?" she finally huffed. "Arlo Epps is a growed man. He can just take care a hisself."

"But he might get drownded," I insisted.

"Hah!" was all she said.

I wasn't surprised at her acting so hateful toward him. They'd had an argument that morning, as usual. I'd heard them rumbling at one another through the walls. It went on longer than most and I'd begun to wonder if there'd be any breakfast at all, then he'd jumped into the river. As a matter of fact, there wasn't no breakfast, but I never really noticed because I was so worried about Uncle Arlo.

Come midafternoon, me avoiding chores to watch him fight that current, still figuring him to collapse any second, I determined to rescue my uncle. Without asking permission, I pulled our boat, the Packard Prow Special, out from the shed and dragged her to the river's bank.

The Special was this old wooden dinghy that Uncle Arlo he'd took for a dowsing job years before. She'd never looked too great but, in spite of her one-lunged motor, he'd been able to use her on that river without no trouble. What give the Special class, though, was that Packard hood ornament Arlo'd wired to her prow. He'd traded for it at this yard sale and he kept it all the time shined, something that really ate at Aunt Maize Bee. She said it just showed how foolish he was. She said that all the time.

Anyways, I launched the boat and managed to maneuver it into position next to my uncle, that bright ornament pointed upstream toward the canyon. I leaned over to talk to him, but was shocked by what I seen. He was so *white*. I'd always seen his arms from the elbow down, and his face, all real tan, but the rest of him— the part his clothes hid—was the color of a trout's belly, and it seemed like he shimmered in that clear, rushing water like some kinda ghost. It was scary. "Uncle Arlo," I finally called, "Please come in. You'll get drownded for sure."

My uncle he just kept on cruising, his face out of the water every other stroke. His eyes they looked real big and white, but I couldn't tell if he recognized me. "Shall I bring you some dinner?" I yelled. "You gotta eat." He never answered, but those two-tone arms kept stretching, those white eyes turning.

Then he done something that surprised me. This fat stonefly it come bouncing down the water toward him. Just before it reached his face, he twisted his body and snapped the big insect into his mouth. "Crime-in-ently!" I gasped. I surely wasn't gonna mention *that* to Aunt Mazie Bee.

Whenever I chugged the Packard Prow back to shore, I hurried

to the cabin and confronted my aunt. "You *gotta* do something,"
I insisted. "Uncle Arlo'll get drownded for sure."

"He'll no such a thang," she snapped. "Arlo Epps won't act his
age is what he won't. He just wants attention, but what he needs
is to brang some money in this house and stop his durn dreamin'."

"But Aunt Mazie Bee . . ."

"No buts! Now do your chores!"

Well, I stayed up all that night, or tried to—I reckon I mighta
dozed some, leaning against the Special there on the bank. Not
much, though, 'cause in the moonlight I could see him, out there
holding against the current, that white body almost flashing like
a fishing lure, never still. Just about dawn, I snuck in the cabin and
brewed coffee, then filled the old thermos bottle. I knew my uncle
he had to be froze by then and I was determined to force some
hot coffee down him. I carried it to the Special, then bucked the
river's swirl out to Arlo and positioned the boat right next to him.
He didn't pay me no mind. "You gotta drink some coffee," I urged.
"Uncle Arlo, pleeease." He kept pulling against that rushing
water, snapping at the morning's hatch of mayflies. I finally give
up.

That afternoon, a reporter and a photographer from the
Bakersfield newspaper they showed up. My aunt'd called them. "I
thought you wasn't gonna give Uncle Arlo no attention," I hissed
to her out the corner of my mouth.

"Hesh up," she snapped, "or I'll peench a chunk outta you.
Besides, I'm not a-givin' him the kind he wants, I'll tell you that
much. We gotta live some way, don't we?"

That reporter he was a stout gent that chewed on a unlit cigar.
His partner was a little weasel lugging this big, giant camera, and

with a fat bag hanging from one shoulder. He listed whenever he walked.

After my aunt got done telling her story, that reporter he just closed his notebook and put his stub pencil away. "Lady," he said real rough, "you must think we were born yesterday. Nobody could do what you claim your old man's done. We weren't born yesterday, right Earl?"

"Right," agreed the photographer.

"Ask the boy," snapped Maize Bee, unwilling to back down.

The reporter he wiggled his wet cigar at her, then he turned to face me. "Well, boy?" he demanded.

I looked at the ground. "It's true. Honest."

We was standing on the river's bank, maybe a hundred feet from were Uncle Arlo worked against the current. The reporter he stared at that pale form that the rushng water made look like a torpedo, then he asked, "What's that guy wearing?"

I looked at my aunt and she looked at me. "Well, he left in a big hurry," she finally said.

"Yeah, but what's he wearing?"

"Nothin'," she choked.

"Nothing? You mean he's bare-assed?"

"Yeah," I gulped, and my aunt she looked away.

"For Chrissake, Earl, get a picture of that nut!"

"Right," said the photographer.

"What'd you say his name was," asked the reporter, and Aunt Maize Bee she smiled.

The story with a picture was in that next morning's paper and the crowds begun arriving before lunch. My aunt she was ready for them.

Maize Bee stationed herself at the gate in a warped wooden lawn chair we'd salvaged years before from the river. She also had me set up our old card table—that we got cheap at a yard sale—and she put on it a cigar box to hold all the money she planned to collect, plus a can to spit snuff juice into. Across her lap she laid our old single-shot .410 that Uncle Arlo'd swapped for way back when. Finally, she tied on her good sunbonnet and waited. "Ever'body pays, buster," she told the first arrival. "That'll be two-bits." Then she spit into the can, "Ptui!" and give me a I-told-you-so grin.

Whata buncha jokers turned out. While my uncle was struggling out in that water, pick-ups and jalopies and hot rods sped to the fence, and out spilled the darndest specimens I ever seen: mostly young studs with more tattoos per square mile than the state pen. All colors and shapes, sleeves rolled up and sucking on toothpicks, gals parading in bathing suits and shorts, giggling and pointing while boyfriends they scowled at each other.

"Hell, I could swim 'er easy," claimed one old boy that had a pack of cigarettes rolled into a sleeve of his t-shirt, and the crowd cheered. A minute later he was into a fight with another guy that had his sleeves rolled up too, and the crowd surged and tugged for a minute, then cheered some more.

Aunt Maize Bee hardly seemed to notice the goings on. She sat counting quarters and filling that spit can. Once she called, "No rock throwin', buster," and she gestured with her scattergun. The old boy quit flinging stones at Uncle Arlo right now.

A little later, after she'd sold a couple old tires for a dollar and this beat-up bike seat for thirty cents, a great big pot-bellied devil without no shirt on he swaggered up to the doorway of our cabin,

but my aunt never blinked: "Nothin' for sale in there, buster, but you about to buy this .410 shell." She clicked back the hammer, and he lost interest in the cabin. A hour later she sold the lawn chair to a Mexican man for seventy-five cents and took to accepting bids on the card table. I never liked the way she was eyeing the Packard Prow Special.

It was about dark, the crowd finally drifting off, whenever that Cadillac it swooped up to the gate. Out of the driver's seat come this big, tough-looking guy in a suit and tie that went and opened a back door. A short, fat guy—in a suit and tie but with a hat too—he squeezed out. The two of them they paid my aunt—by now she was sitting on a nail keg—then they trooped through what was left of the picnickers and beer drinkers, the crowd kinda opening and staring real quiet as them two passed. Those two looked like they'd showed up at the wrong place.

On the point closest to Uncle Arlo, they stood for a long time, those two, not talking to one another that I could see, their eyes on them two-tone arms, on that two-tone head, and on that ghost of a body in the current. Finally, the fat man he called to my aunt in this high-pitched voice: "Lady, you got a boat we can use?"

Maize Bee's eyes narrowed. "Fer what?"

"For five dollars."

He was speaking my aunt's language, so even before she answered I was trudging to the Special. I knew I'd be ferrying the fat guy. There wasn't room for three in the special, so the fat guy's driver he stayed on shore while the two of us chugged out, the current jerking and pushing us around till I got that hood ornament pointed upstream and we moved toward Uncle Arlo. That bigshot he clung to the boat's sides tight as he could, and I

was half-tempted to dump us both just to keep him away from
Arlo because there was *something* about him. He didn't fit.

Whenever we finally maneuvered alongside my uncle, the fat
guy he raised one hand, signaling me to stop, then grabbed the
boat's side again right away. He watched the swimmer for a long
time, then rasped to me, "How long you say he's been at it, boy?"

"Two days nearly."

"Two days without stopping?"

"Uh-huh."

"Take me back," he ordered. "I seen enough."

Soon as we hit shore, the fat man and his pal they joined Aunt
Maize Bee in the cabin after she give me the .410 along with
orders to make sure nobody got in without paying, and not to take
less than twenty cents for the nail keg. She carried the cigar box
with her.

Half an hour later, my aunt walked the fat man and his pal to
that Cad', shook hands, then come back to the gate as they drove
away. "Well, I sold him," she announced, her hands on her hips,
her chin out, grinning.

"Huh?"

"Your uncle, I sold him to that there Mr. Rattocazano of Wide
World Shows. Your uncle's a-gonna be famous and we're agonna
be rich." she told me real proud.

"But you can't *sell* Uncle Arlo," I protest. "You can't do that!"

"I can so!" she asserted. "Besides, I never exactly sold *him*, I jest
sold that Mr. Rattocazano the right to exhibit him. Course, we
gotta git him declared crazy first, but Mr. Rattocazano says his
lawyer'll take care a that in no time. They'll brang him and the
sher'ff out tomorra."

"The sheriff?"

"To declare Arlo Epps nuts and take him. He's been crazier'n a bedbug for years. Now he can finally support us."

"But Aunt Maize Bee..." I complained.

"You jest hesh!" she snapped. "This here's growed-up's business."

Tired as I was, I couldn't sleep that night for worrying about my uncle, that never hurt a soul, being declared nuts and took to the nuthouse or stuck in some kinda freak show. No sir, was all I could think, not to my uncle you don't. It seemed like to me that Aunt Maize Bee was the one gone crazy.

Before dawn, I crept out to the Packard Prow Special and hit the river. Soon as the engine coughed me out alongside Uncle Arlo—him not looking any different to me than he had that first morning, arms reaching for the water in front of him, head turning regular to breath—I hollered at him, hoping the river's growl would cover my voice. "You gotta come back, Uncle Arlo," I pleaded. "The sheriff's gonna come and take you away. They say you've went crazy." His movements never changed, so I added, "I brung a towel."

His face kept turning, his arms pulling, but I noticed his eyes roll in my direction: He seen me. We seen each other. A real look. So I told him again: "You gotta come in. The sheriff's coming today, and a lawyer too. They'll take you to the nuthouse or the sideshow, one." I extended that towel.

His body it just shimmered in that hurried water, and his arms kept up their rhythm, but the look on his face it changed. Then, sure as anything, he winked at me. That was when I noticed that the Special it was gradually falling behind him. I thought for a

second that the sick old motor was giving up but, no, it sounded the same as always. Then I realized that he was moving upstream, real slow but moving, toward the rapids and that cataract.

I opened the throttle of the Special and caught Arlo, but not for long. We was getting close to those rapids, and he was moving faster all the time. Them two-tone arms they was churning faster and his two-tone face hardly seemed to be sucking air at all as he dug in. The Special was wide open but it was lagging farther and farther behind, so I throttled back the engine to hold even in the current, not wantin' to get into the rapids.

Up ahead, I seen my uncle slide into them, kinda bounce but keep swimming, around curling whirlpools, up swooshing runs, over hidden boulders, not believing what I was seeing with my own eyes, until pretty soon he reached the boiling edge of that cataract. I couldn't hardly breath.

For what seemed like a long, long time he disappeared in the white water and I was scared he'd finally drownded. Then I seen this pale shape shoot up out a the water, looking less like a man at that distance than some fair fish. The current it drove him back, but a second later he come out of that froth again, farther this time, almost over the worst of it, but not quite and he fell back into that terrible foam. I figured him a goner for sure, and I squeezed my eyes closed not wanting to see what happened. A second later, I couldn't resist squinting them open. "Come *on,* Uncle Arlo," I heard myself rooting, "*make* it!"

Then he exploded, a ghost that popped from the cataract like...well, almost like an unsheathed soul, smack into the smooth water above. I couldn't believe it, but I cheered, "Yaaaay!"—my heart pumping like sixty. Whenever I rubbed my

eyes and shook my head, he was stroking up there out of sight into the canyon.

I plooped in the wiggling Special, breathing real heavy, and I wiped my own face with the towel I'd brung for Uncle Arlo. He was away and I was exhausted, so I pointed the Packard Prow toward the bank. Whenever I got to shore, Aunt Maize Bee come out from the cabin. "Where's your uncle at?" she demanded, her eyes searching the river.

"He drownded," I replied.

She glanced from me to the stream and back, made a clucking sound with her mouth, then said, "He *would*."

Death of a Star-Nosed Mole

HE'D BEEN DRINKING WHEN I ARRIVED that evening, not that he was drunk or anything, but you know a thick old guy like Hal always seems to lurch more, to gasp more, to fumble more with his thick fingers, so I knew he was feeling it. I'd been trying to drop by regularly after work in the weeks since Carrie, his wife, had passed away, and I'd often find him in that dim kitchen sipping beer, gazing at the fading wallpaper.

His solitary drinking worried me. I tried to talk him into getting out of his empty house, but usually he wouldn't. That particular evening, to my suprise and pleasure, he agreed to accompany me to a softball game, so I followed him to the hall closet where he was going to grab a sweater. Just as he started to close the door, I heard him murmur, "Would you look at that."

I glanced in seeing nothing at first, then noticed in the closet's darkness what appeared to be a dense lump of shadow in one

corner. Looking more closely, I realized that it was the form of a small beast. Snapping on the light, we both examined the strange little animal—thick gray fur that shuddered irregularly, and a rosy, splayed nose protruding from a bald face. "I'll be damned," Hal said. "Is is a gopher?"

On either side of the face projected thick, fleshy forefeet that looked like pump hands. They were held there almost like a fighter's mitts, high and ready. I thought for a moment before answering him. "No," I finally replied, "I think it's a mole, a star-nosed mole. I saw a picture of one in *National Geographic* once. They're blind, I think."

"I'll be..."

"You ever try to dig one up, a mole I mean? We had one in our garden and I dug damn near to China and never did get him. You never know how deep the earth can be, or how dark. How'd it get in here, I wonder?"

Hal shrugged, "Maybe old Jay the tomcat brought it in. He brings things in sometimes, but never anything like this before."

"Well, unless you want the cat to kill it, we'd better catch it and...well, do something."

Hal walked into the kitchen and returned with a large, plastic pitcher into which he scooped the unresisting animal. We both examined it up close, and Hal finally said, after a deep sigh, "I think I'll keep him awhile. I'll damn sure never get another chance to see one."

"I don't think these guys do too good in captivity," I told him.

He shrugged. "I'll put some dirt in this old terrarium," he explained as he pulled a rectangular glass container from one of the closet's shelves. It had belonged to his son but, like the trophies

and scrapbooks and everything else connected with Timmy, it had been buried in that obscurity for years.

We trooped outside and he shoveled garden soil into the terrarium, then carefully dug for earthworms to add as I'd suggested. "These little guys can really burrow with those front feet," I commented because the mole did just that as soon as it was placed in the terrarium, virtually disappearing as soon as it hit that earth. "That article I read said they locate food with that funny nose," I added.

"Huh," nodded Hal, dropping several worms onto the soil in the glass container. For a moment neither of us said anything, then he suggested, "Let's skip the ballgame. Come on, I've got some beer in the frig'."

I wasn't too keen on him drinking any more, but I knew it was important for him to talk, so I agreed. We seated ourselves in the kitchen and he opened two cans, remarking, "I still can't understand why Tim couldn't even come home for his mother's funeral." It was Tim, not Carrie, who dominated his thoughts.

Tim was their only child. "Are you sure he knew?" This was a litany we'd recited many times since the services for Carrie, and I could have recited Hal's response.

"If he didn't, it was his own fault." The voice hardened and lowered, became almost a growl. "No one forced him to leave."

I said nothing because I didn't remember it quite the way Hal did. I *did* recall the very morning he'd come to work looking haggard and I'd asked what was wrong. "I don't want to talk about it," he'd snapped, so I'd let it go, but at lunch that afternoon, leaning against a truck's shady side, he'd turned toward me and choked, "I'm sorry about this morning, Dutch. It's just that

Timmy's quit the team. He's left school and moved in with some hippies." Looking at his ravaged eyes, I knew there was nothing I could say.

His son had been a starter and a good student at San Francisco State, just as he had at our local high school. He was one of those small boys who tries so hard that he can't be kept out of the lineup. He seemed to retire all the school's Most-Inspirational awards. But his dad had never been completely satisfied. I remember him saying to me when Tim was a high school star, "He never gives a 110%. Never."

"Hal," I'd replied, "nobody can do that. 100%'s the limit."

"Not in *my* family," he had replied without smiling.

After the boy had left college and drifted into the drug scene or music scene or whatever scene was around the Haight-Ashbury in the late sixties, his father had been convinced that he'd been too easy on him. "He's soft," Hal'd asserted, "they all are, Tim and the rest of 'em." There had still been a little communication between them at that time, but after his son moved to Canada to avoid the draft, Hal had been outraged and all contact had ceased. No one in town—including his parents—knew where Tim lived or what he was doing; he was, in a real sense, missing in action, and if his mother had mourned, his father had assumed a chrome veneer—refusing to mention his son's name while he grew increasingly intolerant of the anti-war movement, so much so that all of his friends, including me, went to great lengths to avoid talking about it.

When the U.S. finally pulled out of Vietnam, Hal had insisted not only that we'd lost but that we'd lost because the younger generation was in some mysterious manner flawed. "They can't

give 110% like we did against the Japs," he claimed. I changed the subject.

The funny thing is that for years Hal and Tim had seemed models for the rest of us. They went everywhere together, and Hal never missed one of his son's games. The father had been a good natural athlete himself, but the Depression had denied him the opportunity to compete, so he became his boy's greatest supporter, working to buy him the best of everything, but worried that he might give him too much.

If there was a clue to what finally happened, I think it was that Hal, one of the best guys I've ever known, never talked harshly to anyone except his son. He wasn't mean and it wasn't common for him to chew on Tim, but he just seemed to care so much that at times he couldn't control his...what?...his *passion,* or even understand it. I don't know what else to call it but passion. I guess he was just too involved with his boy.

The closest I ever saw the man come to tears was that time Timmy got lost up at Hobo Hot Springs. A bunch of us who worked for Shell Oil had met up there for a picnic and we were having a big time. Timmy and some other kids wandered down to the river to play and we just forgot them. When the women called everyone to eat, no Timmy.

The funny thing is that Hal and a bunch of us were just talking about his son at the time we realized he was missing. The boy was a standout then in little league baseball, and we were kidding his dad, saying that Tim must've gotten those good genes from his mother's side of the family. He'd chuckled and said, "Or from the milkman." Then Hal had uncharacteristically darkened and added, "I don't know if Tim'll ever get anywhere in baseball, though. He

just doesn't *want* it enough. He doesn't really sacrifice for it." Mind you, we were talking about a twelve-year-old kid.

Anyway, at that very moment, Timmy was missing. We weren't too worried at first, but after looking in all the nearby areas, you could feel everyone thicken; too many people, and not just kids, drowned in the Kern River every summer for us not to consider that possibility. I recall that Carrie had assumed the worst, collapsing in a clutch of women while the rest of us searched ever more frantically.

Just about dusk, a ranger drove his pickup into the parking area where we had assembled to decide what to do next, and out jumped Timmy. He had been out hiking, missed a trail junction, and ended up hiking a couple of miles upstream looking for us. The boy was frightened and exhausted, and he ran directly to his father, who hugged him for a moment, then slapped him hard across the face. "Don't you *ever* do that to us again!" A shaken Hal had sobbed.

The boy'd been stunned, and he staggered back a step, then flew to Carrie while his father, his cheeks streaked with tears, continued raging: "Do you *know* what you've done? Do you *know?*"

But I don't think he was angry at all. I think he was so relieved that he just didn't know how to act. Tim was his everything and he wasn't prepared for those feelings. He was embarrassed at work for the next several days and apologized over and over for the trouble his boy had caused me, although he knew it was no trouble at all. What really bothered him, I think, was his own outburst.

Not that Hal was ever one of those jerks who beats on his wife

or kids. I don't recall ever hearing Tim express any resentment or dislike for his dad the way so many teenagers do. Even though he was an only chld, Timmy never acted spoiled. He was polite without being, you know, sullen—a bright, funny kid who laughed as much at himself as at others. We all liked him and he seemed to idolize his dad.

In fact, it always seemed as though he'd do just about anything for his father. Why, when he was tiny, just a year-and-a-half, two-years-old, Hal used to bring him to work, as proud as he could be of the little guy. He was always rubbing Tim's curly blonde hair, squeezing his fat little hands.

But there was something else he did that always stayed with me. In the course of a visit, Timmy would touch something he wasn't supposed to, nothing of any consequence, just some little baby thing, and Hal wouldn't screech or threaten the way you hear some parents. No, instead he did something curious: He'd say simply, "Bend over, Tim," and that baby would, I swear, right on the spot. His dad would give him a little spank on that upturned bottom, nothing hard ever, then Timmy would cloud up, his little hands rubbing his eyes, and Hal would pat his back, crooning, "Now, now, that didn't hurt." Then he'd turn to us and say, "He's gotta learn."

That baby had to know what would happen when he bent over, but he never hesitated, never failed to do it when his father ordered him to, and Hal never failed to give him a spank. "You gotta be consistent," he once told me. They're never too young to learn." We were young ourselves then, little more than kids, newly married and just starting our families. I know I felt pretty savvy at the time, but now I know I had plenty left to learn, we all did.

That was years ago, another lifetime, it seems like, and we were other people.

Now I sit here with Hal—both of us heavy old men with bare skin shining where hair used to grow, wearing trousers with several more inches around the waist than along the inseams— sipping beer, trying to make sense of all that's gone by so fast. We're hashing and rehashing: Carrie's death, good times at work, the sad state of the nation, the fate of old buddies, and Tim, always Tim. I try to use my family in the conversation to kind of lighten Hal's burden because he keeps returning to old, old business.

Every once in awhile, he brightens: "Remember when Tim stole home against North High and won the championship? That pitcher never had a chance." But mostly it was the repeated questions, "Where did he go wrong? What'd those professors up at San Francisco State do to him?"

My old friend seems so shaken that, when he finally falls asleep at the table, I call my wife and tell her that I'm going to spend the night, see that he gets a decent breakfast, and bring him to our house the next day. I help him into bed, then curl myself up on the living room couch rather than Tim's old bed because I want to be alert in case Hal awakens and decides to raid the beer locker.

I was suddenly alert just before six, Hal lurching through the living room. "Hey," I call, and he stops and blinks, swaying there like some heavy beast just out of hibernation.

I roll off the couch—my back aching—"Let me get us some coffee started," I suggest.

"Coffee?" he blinks again, then he seems to focus on me. "Sure. That sounds good."

I put water on to boil, then sneak into the bathroom for a necessary stop. When I return, Hal is standing over Tim's old terrarium, staring into it. "It died," he says to me.

I join him and see on top of the soil the body of the star-nosed mole, its pale hands still, its rosy nose unmoving. Neither of us says anything, but Hal reaches into the glass box and strokes the animal's thick gray coat and touches a plump forefoot. He shudders, withdraws his hand, and gazes away toward the kitchen window where early sunlight is just showing. After a moment, he turns toward me and, out of the blue, he implores, "Why didn't I ever kiss him?"